EBURY PRESS

GOBIND

Harinder S. Sikka is currently group director, strategic business, Piramal Group. After graduating from Delhi University, he joined the Indian Navy. He was commissioned in January 1981 and took premature retirement in 1993 as a lieutenant commander.

He recently produced a film, *Nanak Shah Fakir*, which won acclaim at the Cannes, Toronto and Los Angeles international film festivals. The film won three national awards, including the Nargis Dutt Award for best feature film on national integration.

GOBIND

SUBMARINERS ARE A SPECIAL BROTHERHOOD
EITHER ALL COME TO THE SURFACE
OR NO ONE DOES

HARINDER S. SIKKA

EBURY PRESS
An imprint of Penguin Random House

EBURY PRESS

Ebury Press is an imprint of the Penguin Random House group of companies whose addresses can be found at global.penguinrandomhouse.com

Published by Penguin Random House India Pvt. Ltd
4th Floor, Capital Tower 1, MG Road,
Gurugram 122 002, Haryana, India

Penguin
Random House
India

First published in Ebury Press by Penguin Random House India 2024

10 9 8 7 6 5 4 3 2 1

This is a work of fiction. Names, characters, places and incidents are either the product of the author's imagination or are used fictitiously and any resemblance to any actual person, living or dead, events or locales is entirely coincidental.

ISBN 9780143464327

Typeset in Adobe Caslon Pro by Manipal Technologies Limited, Manipal
New Delhi

www.penguin.co.in

To my parents and Mr Ajay G. Piramal

1

March 1985

'Run, Gobind, run, run . . . faster, faster!'

Two bare, mud-stained feet scrambled through a dusty field in a small village on the periphery of Patna, the birthplace of Guru Gobind Singh. They were chasing a tennis ball but in vain. The ball rolled towards the boundary marked with chalk powder amidst the applause of the school students who were scattered along the white marker. The runner made a last-ditch effort and dove to grab the ball before it crossed the white line, but this left dust marks and stains on his only school uniform. Brushing his clothes with his hands, Gobind picked up the ball, threw it back and then looked sheepishly at his team members, well aware that his reactions on the field were slow.

'Well done. Keep it up! Let the ball run freely each time. You're so good at this!' The sarcasm-laced words

from one of the spectators weren't lost on Gobind and that showed up on his face. The acid tone seared him from within and his eyes reflected the flames of anger. He first glanced at the teenager who was standing with a couldn't-care-less attitude and then at the others who were openly commenting on his untidy uniform and muddy feet. Amidst boos, hoots and free-flowing insulting barbs from the rich brats, Gobind began his long walk towards the pitch, mentally preparing himself to face the ire of his teammates as well.

Exiting the school an hour later, he turned one of the several taps installed along the school's boundary wall. He washed his hands and splashed water on his hot face several times. Then, in the cup of his palms, he took the cool water and lowered his head to gulp the liquid. He knew that even though his team had lost the match for a host of other reasons, he would be targeted as the villain for the defeat because of his humble family background. It was easier for everyone to make him the scapegoat. Quenching his thirst, Gobind began a slow, defeated walk towards his home. He began worrying about facing the wrath of his father as he walked. His mid-term academic report card carried so many red circles that he wanted to forget that he ever took the test. However, there was little he could do now. The entrance to his house loomed in front of him.

Pushing the door open, Gobind stepped into the small verandah. He began pushing down the long handle of the handpump installed in the outer courtyard. With little effort, water came out, gushing. Cleaning his feet, arms

and legs, he waited briefly to see if there was any reaction from his parents sitting inside the room. Observing the silence, he wiped his face with his hands and walked into the small, dimly lit but neatly kept one-room home. Sitting on a cot in front was his father, Ranjit Singh. His mother, Amrita, was standing close by, swinging the hand-held fan and almost willing and directing the air to her husband's face. Their eyes were glued on to the report card.

Ranjit Singh looked up for a brief moment and then glanced at Amrita before venting his pent-up anguish. 'Do you know, Gobind, what it takes to earn two square meals a day? Do you have any idea how many sacrifices are being made to send you to a good school? Your mother has only two sarees. She refuses to buy another. I walk 10 kilometres daily to save every penny to pay for your school. Despite all these efforts and sacrifices, you bring such pathetic results. What should I do with you?' Then, without looking up, Ranjit flung the report card at Gobind. The double folded sheet of yellow paper took to air and swung open. It then floated around the room like an unmanned glider, took a U-turn and landed on the floor exactly where Gobind was standing.

He stood in silence, watching his mother now vigorously turning the fan on its pivot, to increase its rotation speed. The wooden swivel creaked and hissed, adding to the growing lines of anger on the father's forehead. The additional gush of air did little to cool Ranjit's temper. Being a daily wager, his only mission was to educate his son. The report card had come as a

dampener to his aspirations and taken the wind out of his sails, dashing the hope that he had been nurturing for long. He looked at his son helplessly and then glanced towards Amrita. 'Has he eaten?' The anger in his voice showed no sign of receding.

'No, he hasn't,' came the quiet response. And even though her voice was low, it carried her pain, fear and helplessness.

Ranjit's facial expression softened. He stood up from the cot and sat on the floor while Amrita rushed to the tiny makeshift kitchen to fetch plates. They ate in silence. The food was simple, but Gobind was so hungry that he emptied his plate even before his father could begin eating. This pained his parents more because it made them realize their inability to adequately feed their growing son. They glanced at each other before Ranjit turned towards his son. His anger had receded.

Lowering his voice, he said, 'Gobind, your father is not a well-to-do man. He is a daily wager who can't even feed his family properly. Lack of education forced me to accept small, low-paying jobs. As a result, we all have suffered. Like a solid pillar, your mother has stood by me, and we gave up everything just to ensure that you receive the best education. She stitches clothes, and I work overtime to make sure that our son gets a good education so that he can build a great future for himself. Son, it's not shameful to be poor. But it's hugely challenging and demanding. I want you to remember that this amazing journey called "life" comes without a map. We have to search for our own

routes to reach our destination. And the sooner you set your goals, the better your journey ahead shall be.'

Ranjit's voice had, by then, lost its anger-laced, high-pitched tone. Reluctantly Gobind accepted one chapati from his father's share, rolled it with the remaining onions and ginger on his plate and swallowed it quickly. He waited till his parents had finished their meal and then stepped out into the courtyard. Under the full-moon-lit sky, he leaned against the wall and stared at the vast fields till his eyes came to rest on the big haveli that was shining under the silvery rays. His serious and tense face eased up. Then, he turned back to his own little home and pulled out a small cot from beneath his father's bed. Spreading a thick cotton sheet on top of it, he lay on it, resting his head on the wooden frame. He was tired, but sleep had long deserted him. His father's words began playing in his mind: 'It's not a crime to be poor, Gobind. But to not have a mission is an unpardonable offence for you are being unjust to those who are ever so willing to sacrifice their all, just to see you soar high.'

He ran his fingers through his long hair that was tied up on top of his head. His face bore signs of fatigue. For the first time, he had felt the depth of pain and sorrow in his father's voice. He tossed and turned, and then lay with his face towards the slowly churning fan on the ceiling— the reason why his mother still relied on the hand-held fan. Even though he tried his best to sleep, his eyes remained wide open.

Then, gently, without making much noise, Gobind sat up, pushed the thin sheet away and sat in a meditative posture. He had often heard his father recite the magical

words that would miraculously energize him. His lips began moving slowly, murmuring the same prayer he had heard so often. His eyes were closed.

The words emerged effortlessly:

Deh Shiva bar mohe ihai
shubh karman te kabhun na taro . . .

(O great power, give me the boon, so that I may never shirk away from doing good deeds . . .)

He sat motionlessly for a few minutes reciting the prayer and then lay back on the cot. He recalled the story that his mother had narrated to him a thousand times.

Guru Gobind Singh, the tenth Sikh guru, was born in Patna, Bihar, on 22 December 1666. Gobind Rai, as he was named by his parents, stood against the tyranny and brutality of the then Mughal Emperor Aurangzeb, who was hell bent on forcibly converting the entire Hindu race to Islam. In addition to being a dynamic and courageous warrior, Guru Gobind Singh was also a spiritual leader with an enormous following. At his command, thousands of Hindu families happily gave away their eldest sons to become Sikhs (disciples), who fought against the Mughals. A frustrated Aurangzeb suffered humiliating defeat at the hands of a small army of Gobind's warriors, who stood their ground despite facing enormous challenges.

'We are proud of our heritage and the sacrifices our forefathers have made many centuries ago. We have named

you after the Guru so that you are blessed with the same courage to stand up against all the odds and emerge as a hero. Our wishes and prayers are all dependent on your efforts and we hope to see them fructify, sooner than later,' his mother would repeat each time after the story.

Gobind turned to one side slowly. There were signs of mental fatigue when he did so as if he was doing it with great effort. He had never heard his father speak to him in such a distress-filled voice. He kept looking at the ceiling as if to allow the transformation that was taking place within him to sink in completely. The ceiling fan was no longer visible, his vision was blurred and thoughts stopped coming to him. Then, as if by a miracle, a calmness overpowered him and eased out his worries, reflecting the birth of determination from within. The boy in Gobind was turning into a man and preparing to take on the world on his own terms.

2

As the sun emerged from the distant horizon, the fields too began changing colour. The rapidly strengthening sun rays turned brighter with every passing minute, turning the dark and dense looking crops into a lush green landscape. Tiny golden-yellow flowers on top of the crops looked as if each plant had been knighted with a golden crown by mother nature. All kinds of birds emerged from their deep slumber and filled the atmosphere with a burst of chirpy sounds. The entire village was soon bathed in different hues. Not to be left behind, the animals too began walking around their territories, marking, urinating on every pole, tree and bush. The farmers too began making a beeline on the snake-like thin track to their respective fields. Their farming tools hung from their shoulders like weapons saddled on the shoulders of soldiers enroute to the battlefield. Nature in its full glory was like a beacon of peace, love and tranquility all round.

Gargling and spitting the water out, Ranjit Singh accepted from his wife an old piece of cloth that was once a garment, re-stitched to serve as a face napkin. While handing it back to Amrita, he looked at her inquiringly, 'Where's Gobind?'

'Oh, he has already left for the fields. Says he will come back in three hours and go to school afterwards,' she replied.

The cloth napkin slipped out of Ranjit's hand and fell on the wet floor between them.

'Which fields?' he asked, his face filled with shock and surprise.

'To work in Bihari Lal's field. Before leaving home, he told me that he wished to earn while he studied. I couldn't stop him. He just left without discussing it further.'

Ranjit was speechless. His young, school-going teenage son had taken a decision to work part-time, without even consulting his father.

'I don't know what to make of all this. Working part time isn't wrong. In fact, I am happy for this will inculcate discipline in him. But all of a sudden? I will ask Bihari ji what's he up to.'

Amrita bent down to pick the cloth from the floor. Then, flapping it in the air repeatedly, she tried to remove the excess water it had absorbed from the wet floor and flung it on the clothesline to dry. She turned towards her husband and looked straight into his eyes. 'Maybe we should leave him alone. Let him discover himself. He didn't sleep well. He even sat up on the cot in the middle of night to say his prayers. He was unsettled last night after

your stern talk. But he looked different this morning and very charged up when I met him, before he left quickly. There's this visible change in him that I have never seen before. I am happy and worried.'

'Prayer? Gobind? And how do you know he has changed?' Ranjit's face was now filled with confusion.

'Because I am his mother.'

Ranjit's eyes followed Amrita as she went inside the room. Then, wiping his hands on the cloth napkin that Amrita had just hung, he turned his attention outside. He lifted himself up on his toes and looked in the direction of the large haveli with vast green fields where his son was supposed to be working. His eyes scanned the horizon but couldn't see Gobind. Turning back, he walked inside to find Amrita standing at the entrance, watching her husband.

'Please stop worrying. You'll get late for work. Get ready; I will get your breakfast. Your tiffin is also ready. Please don't forget to take it along.'

Amrita's affection-filled instructions relaxed Ranjit to some extent. Stepping into the room, he sat down on the floor while Amrita served him breakfast. It was the same food that he had eaten last night. He ate in silence. But his mind was racing in many directions while Amrita rotated the hand-held fan on its swivel. Before leaving home for work, he stood before the lord's picture hung on the wall, joined his palms and murmured so softly that even his own ears couldn't hear his own words. 'With your permission, dear lord, I wish to go to work. It's a new day, an amazing one at

that. I want to thank you from the bottom of my heart. Only you, dear Guru Gobind, can help my son, Gobind.'

Amrita stood watching her husband in admiration. She couldn't hear what Ranjit was saying, yet she could very easily guess every word that he had uttered. Customarily, she also murmured the same prayer. While joyous to see her husband in a happy mood, she noticed a change in Ranjit's prayers. Her lips stopped abruptly because they were not in sync with her husband's. Ranjit had added more words to the prayer, she observed. It was longer than the one he said daily. She smiled to herself but decided to stay quiet and followed him to the veranda.

Seeing him off at the gate, she rushed back to where Ranjit had stood moments ago. She looked at the picture frame. 'Dear lord, please grant my husband whatever he has asked for. Kindly take care of him and Gobind. They are all I have. Thank you for your mercy!' Tiny drops of tears appeared and settled beneath her eyelids. Wiping them quickly, she turned to find Ranjit standing at the door, watching her intently. Stepping forward, he hugged her warmly, picked up the tiffin box and went away without uttering a word. The tall, lanky old man tried his best, but couldn't hide his emotions. The deity inside the frame looked pleased too, or so Amrita felt.

* * *

Gobind was quite unaware of the upheaval his changed behaviour had caused back home. Ploughing the fields

with the help of two strong bullocks named Hira and Moti, he went about his business in a calm and composed manner. Holding the reins in his hands, he stood firmly on the plough as the two big bulls pulled effortlessly. His entire body went up and down like that of a surf-board rider navigating tidal waves.

Hira and Moti were trained bullocks accustomed to the drill. Although the field was large, they seemed to be well aware of the lay of the land and also where their master's territory ended. After walking in straight lines till the end of the territory, the bulls took a U-turn without even so much of a nudge, leaving a beautiful pattern on the six-feet-wide carved out earth. Anticipating the sharp turn, Gobind skillfully balanced himself. Every muscle on his naked chest coordinated in unison, supporting him to maintain his posture on the thin platform even as he continued to fish out sheaf of papers one by one from his back pocket. This was the first time ever that he was preparing for his tests.

Not far away, standing in a spacious balcony was Meera, the beautiful, petite daughter of Bihari Lal, the landlord of almost half the village. She watched the handsome teenager at work with keen interest. Admiration was writ large on her face as she watched the young man engrossed in studying while sweating it out on the fields. Holding a porcelain tea mug in her hands, she kept gazing at Gobind as he shuffled the papers, skillfully balancing his athletic body on the plough.

Gobind worked nonstop for two hours and then guided the animals to the barn. Shaking their heads, the

bullocks responded to his gesture and waited eagerly to be unhooked from the pulling gear. Their heads kept going up and down, making the tiny bells wrapped around their necks on a cord ring in unison. And soon, as they were released, the two big, stout animals rushed to the water bay and put their heads into the stream flowing through the long and narrow tube-well hose.

Gobind rushed to the haystack shed, gathered the feed in a small tow cart and spread it on to the troughs near the water bay. He then went to the bullocks and patted them on their backs as if to thank them for their hard work. With a hard jute brush, he scrubbed them down one by one and rinsed their white skin using the same hose. The water splashed back on to his own body repeatedly, but it didn't seem to bother him. An amazed Meera witnessed the drama unfolding in front of her eyes. Gobind's muscular shoulders, arms and shapely body frame attracted her young and innocent heart.

Just then, a young maid walked into the balcony from the large wooden door and stood close to her. Without looking up, Meera handed her the mug and asked in a polite, gentle tone, 'Who's that boy over there, Pushpa?' The maid looked up, smiled and replied, 'Oh, that's Gobind, Amrita's son. He lives nearby. His father is a daily wager. Perhaps, he needs money for his school fee and is, therefore, working in your fields.' Meera didn't respond but kept admiring the young man who was freely and lovingly mingling with the animals.

Finishing his chores, Gobind picked up his T-shirt from the hedge and put his head through the narrow opening of

the collar. As his head emerged through the garment, his eyes met Meera's. He had heard about her and was aware of her beauty but had never seen her in person. Slipping his arms one by one into the T-shirt, he tried in vain to move his eyes away from the angel in front of him. With some effort, he embarrassingly turned his head towards the soft mud track leading to his home and began running, fully aware that the pair of beautiful eyes that had just met his own were following him all the way.

Amrita stood at the door, holding the same piece of cloth that her husband had used a few hours ago, along with a copper jug filled with water to the brim. Not accustomed to such a reception, Gobind hesitatingly accepted the jug, splashed water on his face almost in the same manner that he had seen his father do on numerous occasions. He dried his face and hung the cloth back on the line. 'Thanks, Ma,' he uttered and rushed into the house.

Amrita stood glued to the place, trying to grasp and absorb deep within everything she had just witnessed, admiring the transition taking place in her teenage son. It was the most beautiful moment for the mother in her to witness the one change that every woman always longs for, that of her child flapping his wings and testing his muscles before taking his first flight. Her son was transforming into a handsome and responsible young man. His broad shoulders were curved at both ends like a bow, supporting the muscular chest that narrowed at the waist. She could see the sweat that had drenched his T-shirt after the toil of the day. He had put in effort to earn his share of bread.

Closing her eyes briefly, she looked up at the blue skies. 'Thank you, Waheguru, for coming to my hut last night. I am ever so very indebted to you.' As she walked inside, a whiff of fresh air flapped the napkin hanging on the clothesline. The cloth swung up and down ever so gently, as if acknowledging her prayer. And so did the cycle of time that went flying past, like an offshore wind changing course.

* * *

Gobind and Meera began exchanging looks and an occasional smile but nothing more. Meera lived in a protected environment and was always escorted to school in a car. She had a few friends who visited her on select occasions, but she never stepped out of the haveli by herself. Bihar wasn't known to be the easiest of the places to live for the rich. Kidnapping for ransom was a common practice, often with political patronage, and had almost acquired the status of a booming cottage industry for the kidnappers. Bihari Lal, therefore, had good reasons to be extra vigilant. However, his well-armed, watchful security guards could not stop the two young, innocent hearts from getting closer.

Their attraction grew with every passing day. Meera began dreaming of her life with Gobind without the wealth and status of her father. The gigantic horns of Hira–Moti served as message boards for the two to communicate. It all first began with a small caricature that Meera painted on

the bullock horns and penned a small message beneath for Gobind to decipher. While bathing the two bulls the next morning after field work, Gobind noticed the colourfully painted sign and the text that read: 'Work if you must, but do take a break.' He looked towards the balcony to find a smiling Meera expecting him to respond.

After wiping the horns clean, he scribbled a small message in English: 'Am grateful. But like these beautiful animals, I too have little choice.' His innocent response touched her heart and she began conversing with him using the unique platform. English became the chosen language for no one at the haveli was educated enough to understand the text. Whenever they were within visual range, Meera would wave at him in a way that looked like she was pushing her hair back. And while doing so, her palm would swiftly run through her long, dense tresses. Gobind would simply smile in return and shyly put his head down.

On a day when her father had gone out to Patna for routine business, Meera directed the two bullocks to be brought to the fields. She wanted to feel the effort that Gobind put in while ploughing the soil. The field workers objected to her adventure, as they were scared of facing Bihari Lal's wrath. But they couldn't do much against her firm resolve. She worked on the field and even dug the raw ground with a shovel. In less than an hour, her entire body was drenched in sweat. She was exhausted, but her eyes were filled with tears, because now she knew the hardship Gobind was enduring daily.

Pushpa was extremely loyal to Meera. She soon realized her lady's growing attraction for Gobind. She devised many ways to communicate Meera's messages and earned her confidence. She also began interacting with Gobind and learnt about his passion for music and playing drums. Following Gobind, she found his makeshift platform at the back of the village temple, where Gobind had cleverly set up a small but effective workstation using the spare construction material lying in the backyard. He studied under the temple lights for long hours and when exhausted, he de-stressed by playing on a variety of disposable drums and tin plates that were creatively installed by him using thin bamboo poles. She decided to play the matchmaker and worked out a plan for the two to meet in person.

On the pretext of visiting the temple, she escorted Meera but ensured that her security guards waited outside the complex. Sneaking through the small exit at the rear, she made Meera stand in front of her love for the first time. Gobind was hesitant and quite scared at first to face a shy but confident-looking Meera standing before him. Despite Pushpa's prodding, he uncomfortably kept looking at Meera but said nothing. Realizing his predicament, Meera stepped forward and broke the ice. 'Some friendships seem meaningless, but they make life invaluable.' The softness and humility in her voice took the winds out of Gobind's sails. Hesitatingly, he accepted her extended hand and gently held it while looking into her eyes. 'Thank you so much, Meera. I have nothing to offer, but I feel honoured to see you here.'

Meera looked around at the small but neatly kept shack. In place of a roof, there was a large rolled-down canvas cover supported by several long bamboo poles. A solitary bulb hung over a mid-sized writing table facing the temple wall. Its light was good enough for the entire shack to be adequately illuminated. A few racks nailed along the wall were filled with books and stationery. Meera went around the room and took a closer look at the books on the makeshift shelf. And as she picked up one, the entire rack came crashing down. 'Oh, I am so sorry,' she exclaimed apologetically. Gobind smiled and joined her in rearranging the books. 'Not your fault, Meera. It's not fixed properly. I didn't have time. Can I get you water?' Then, without waiting for her response, he went towards the other end and opened the earthen pot, filled a glass of water and neatly placed it on a plate. He then covered the pot with the same cloth and carried the plate to Meera.

Amused but impressed by the quick drill, she picked up the glass and drank some before putting the copper tumbler on the table. 'You know something, Gobind,' she began, 'I had heard, read and seen all this in books and films. But this is the first time I am witnessing it with my own eyes. Your dedication, hard work and passion are unimaginable. You look so much at peace with yourself, yet I know many who possess every comfort that money can buy but remain discontent. I am so happy to have met you. Thank you.' Gobind smiled sheepishly but said nothing. He kept looking at her, admiring her beauty. They sat on the mattress on the floor and chatted till Pushpa knocked

and entered without waiting to be called in. 'I think we should go now. Your security guards are getting anxious.' Meera stood up quickly and the two departed, but not before she held Gobind's hands in hers. 'We shall meet again soon. Take care.'

They met regularly thereafter and became an inseparable couple. Gobind's drumbeats became more melodious and rhythmic. Sitting far away in her palatial haveli, the rhythmic sounds of the drumbeats filled Meera's ears and heart with peace and calm. While Bihari Lal felt proud to see his daughter spend quality time at the temple every evening, Pushpa ensured a variety of eatables were carried by Meera in the name of offerings to the lord. Despite the hustle and bustle at the temple on most days, they managed to keep their meetings a well-guarded secret under the pretext of conducting prayers in an adjacent arena within the premises that was not open to the public. The old priest too played along. Having seen Gobind's determination to excel against all odds, he accepted Meera's love for the young man as God's blessing.

3

Ram Dyal Sharma was the celebrated headmaster of one of the best schools in Patna. Situated on the outskirts of the city, the school provided boarding and lodging facilities along with a foolproof security system to its students. As a result, the school had a fair share of children from the elite class of the city. They were mostly the children of politicians, judges, bureaucrats and businessmen. For many decades, Ram Dyal had run the school with a great degree of success, raising the bar of all-round performance by many a notch. A hands-on administrator, he seldom let the grass grow beneath his feet and had a reputation of being able to foretell the capabilities of every student to a great degree of accuracy.

However, on that day, his body language and facial expressions displayed signs of deep shock, surprise and awe. He was pacing up and down and scratching his head repeatedly. His dishevelled hair and wrinkled forehead bore

the signs of bewilderment, over-shadowing his personality. Lying scattered on top of the large, shiny wooden desk were numerous English dailies and other vernacular newspapers. Standing with joined palms in front was Ranjit Singh, who looked equally bemused, tense and fearful. Picking up one of the newspapers in his left hand, Ram Dyal went closer to him and politely gestured with his right hand to his worried-looking visitor. He paused briefly before urging Ranjit to be seated. But the poor father who wasn't accustomed to such courtesies and generosities stayed put.

The headmaster went closer and held Ranjit Singh gently without letting go of the newspaper as if it were a prized possession. Bowing slightly, he greeted Ranjit with great respect and nudged him to accept the offer. Ranjit was left with no choice. Even as his hands trembled slightly, he kept them joined while he sat on a chair. With an awkward pause, he looked up at the headmaster with troubled eyes and waited with bated breath, expecting to hear the bomb shell drop at any moment. Both his legs were shaking as he began gearing up to listen to the reasons behind him being summoned by the principal.

'Sir, would you like to have tea, some juice or coffee?' began Ram Dyal in a humble tone. For Ranjit, the words came as a double whammy. He was now certain that something extremely wrong had transpired. With great difficulty, he managed to murmur. 'Sir, I am fine. Thank you. I apologize for whatever my son, Gobind, has done. I shall make sure he does not repeat it again. May I humbly request you to kindly pardon him this one time? My wife

and I work very hard to make him study in this school and have cleared all his dues till date. Please have mercy on him. My son is our only hope.'

It was now the headmaster's turn to be taken aback. The worn-out collar of Ranjit's shirt bore ample signs of excessive wear and tear. His eyes were filled with fatigue and his face was lit with fear, tension and anxiety. Up until then, so deeply engrossed was Ram Dyal in his own thought process that he had no time to decipher the mental state of the parent he had summarily called to the school. Joining his palms apologetically, the headmaster bowed low and held Ranjit's palms gently. 'There is no reason for you to worry, dear Ranjit Singh ji. On the contrary, the school management is extremely grateful to you and your wife for bestowing upon us a rare honour by admitting Gobind here. Your ward has brought laurels to this institution. He has created history! On behalf of the school, I wish to express our deep gratitude and sincere thanks to you and your better half.'

A dumbfounded Ranjit was clueless and kept staring at the headmaster. The principal reached out to the call bell and pressed it hard. The peon came running almost instantly and stood motionless. He knew Ranjit well, so looked surprised to see him seated in the plush chair enjoying the headmaster's hospitality. Without looking at him, Ram Dyal ordered, 'Please bring a glass of hot milk immediately.' The peon was taken aback, shock and disbelief clear on his face, as if the directive was for someone else. He had never heard his master order a glass of hot milk before. Ram Dyal

looked at him, smiled and repeated in a polite but firm tone. 'One glass of hot milk please.'

The peon sprang into action. 'Yes, sir,' came a quick response as he exited the spacious office in a hurry.

He pulled a chair and sat opposite Ranjit without letting go off his trembling hands. Wearing a joyous look, the gleeful headmaster began. His voice carried excitement, happiness and humility, but his eyes expressed guilt and pain, realizing that he had unknowingly caused mental agony to his visitor. He began in a gracious manner. 'This is a sheer miracle, Ranjit Singh ji. In my thirty years of teaching experience, I have never ever seen or heard anyone bring in such fantastic results. Gobind has scored a hundred out of hundred in every subject. He has become a role model not only to our district but to the entire state. No one has ever scored such high marks. He has done the unthinkable. He has broken all records.' He paused and looked for Ranjit's reaction.

Seeing him still dumbfounded, he continued, 'By this one single act, Gobind has put our school on the map of the country. My office is flooded with calls from VIPs and journalists. Every citizen in Bihar wants to know more about your brilliant son, Gobind. People are inquiring about his parents, his family background and even going to the extent of checking what he eats. He has done the impossible. And, above all, he has taken us all by complete surprise. What did you do to bring in such a fantastic change in a boy who, till not too long ago, was just an ordinary, below-average student?'

Ranjit was speechless. With shaking hands, he picked up the glass of water from the table and gulped it down. Mustering strength, he looked at the tall figure of the headmaster sitting in front him. He was still uncertain of what he had said at length. His eyes glanced at the newspaper, and he saw an old picture of his son on the front page of an English daily. Beneath the photo was inscribed in bold letters, 'Son of a Daily Wager Creates History. Gobind Shines for Bihar.' Another newspaper in a vernacular language read, 'Gobind Shows the Way, Sets an Unprecedented Record.'

With trembling hands, Ranjit picked up the newspapers from the desk and looked closely at the pictures to ascertain if they actually matched with that of his son's. He couldn't read and did not have an explanation to offer. Instead, he gently folded and pushed the papers closer to his chest and wrapped his hands over them as if they were holy books. Ram Dyal Sharma kept observing every tiny move that Ranjit was making. Like the pleasantly shocked father in front, he too had completely failed to see the potential of his most outstanding student. And that hurt his pride even more. Guilt ridden, the headmaster was sparing no effort to undo his mistake by giving a VVIP treatment to Ranjit.

The peon came rushing in, carrying a tray with a glass of milk, which he placed on the table. The steam emerging from the glass indicated that its contents were as hot as directed by his boss. Ram Dyal picked the glass from the tray and respectfully offered it to Ranjit. Awestruck, the peon looked with utter disbelief at his boss. Without letting

go of the newspapers, Ranjit accepted the glass from Ram Dyal's hand and wrapped the cotton cloth hanging from his shoulder around it. He looked again at the school head for reassurance that the milk indeed was meant for him and began sipping it slowly. Ram Dyal waited patiently. Smiling broadly, he humbly kept urging Ranjit to accept his hospitality. Looking at the numerous threads that were sticking out of Ranjit's shirt collar, Ram Dyal felt a pang of guilt. He had realized that his message had been inadvertently given to Ranjit in a wrong manner.

After a few sips, Ranjit mustered some courage. His hands too steadied, helping him gain confidence. He began softly, 'Sahab, Amrita, my wife, tells me that it is all due to the visit of Sat Kartar to our home.' Placing the glass back on the table, Ranjit waited for the next question that came almost instantly. 'And where can I meet Sat Kartar, sir?' Ranjit paused, looked confused and overwhelmed by the headmaster's humility and searched for the right words. A thick layer of milk had spread around his lips. Wiping it off with the same shoulder cloth, he said, 'Amrita says that Sat Kartar is everywhere and can be found with prayers.'

Despite being a seasoned administrator, Ranjit's innocent and simple response took Ram Dyal by complete surprise. Joining his palms, he bowed again, congratulated Ranjit and complimented him for the rare feat that Gobind had achieved. He walked with Ranjit out of his room and then, in the spur of the moment, decided to escort him all the way till the school gate. Without bothering to acknowledge courtesies, greetings and bows from the workers, teachers

and students, the headmaster stayed focused on his special guest. He stopped a few times enroute to show him the beautifully maintained lawns and other artefacts and showered every courtesy befitting a VVIP, much to the surprise of the onlookers and staff. The peon ran ahead and whispered to the guard who, in turn, shut the smaller entry-exit door and hurriedly pushed open the big iron gate. The headmaster held Ranjit's palms again.

'Sir, I am truly honoured to meet you. I am also terribly sorry for the inconvenience caused to your family. May I request you to graciously grant me permission to visit your home with my wife?' Ranjit felt overwhelmed by the request. Joining his palms, he quickly responded in a polite tone. 'It's your own house, sir. We live in a small cottage, which isn't befitting your stature. But it will be our honour to receive you as per your convenience.' Ranjit paused and glanced at the newspapers he held under his left armpit and asked, 'Sir, I have a request to make. May I please take these papers home?'

Ram Dyal smiled and promptly replied, 'Of course, sir, you can,' even though he knew that Ranjit wouldn't be able to read its contents. The newspapers were no less than invaluable trophies that would become a memoir for the rest of their lives.

Walking back on the narrow pathway leading to his home, Ranjit felt elated. He was emotionally charged and so were his feet that were picking up pace with every forward step. Be it the lush green fields on his left or the scores of women engaged in daily chores in their respective

hutments on his right, everything failed to draw his attention. His mind wandered back to the talk he had had with the headmaster. To him, his daily work and chores were always like worship for that was all he had learnt. Yet, he had ended up speaking about 'Sat Kartar', the one lord, with a certain degree of authority to an educated and highly acclaimed person, who, as a consequence, wished to visit his tiny home with his wife. Where would he make them sit, what would he offer them and how would Amrita react? He kept wondering.

He was also aware that Amrita would be equally tense and praying till he reached home. At least, for now, he wasn't bothered about the half-day leave that would cause him a wage loss. He had actually prepared himself for the worst. Poverty often drives negativity and apprehension as the first response of the poor. Holding the newspapers close to his chest with both hands was straining his shoulders, but he kept increasing his pace, wanting to reach home as soon as possible. Many villagers glanced at him, wondering what valuables were wrapped in the papers he was holding so very dearly.

As Ranjit neared his cottage, he saw the tall and slim silhouette of Amrita at the far end of the dusty road. She too had seen her husband. She had stepped out and now stood in the middle of the pathway, something that she had never done before. She was equally tense and waited eagerly to hear the reason behind the summons. As Ranjit came closer, their eyes met. Amrita's heart was pounding; her eyes stayed glued on her husband's face, as if trying to

extract any clues from his facial expressions. A few women from the neighbourhood too came out, eager to know the reason behind her changed behaviour.

Ranjit was overwhelmed by what had transpired, but he somehow was able to maintain composure. He walked past Amrita without accepting the copper jug and rushed into the sanctity of the four walls of his home. His sweaty face was telling a story that Amrita was unable to decipher. She followed him, almost sprinting the short distance, dropping the water jug on the way. The water splashed across the veranda as the rolling metal jug fell with a loud clang, the sound resonating in their courtyard.

Entering the room, she saw him sitting on the cot, breathing heavily. Sweat droplets were dripping from his face. Then, he looked up, smiling and excited. He pulled out the now slightly damp newspapers from under his arm, his hands trembling a little as he held them. Without letting her husband fully recover from the long walk back home, she took seat on a small stool opposite him, held both his hands in her own and looked directly at him.

'What happened?' she began. 'Why are you so tense? Where's Gobind? Why did they call you to the school? What have they done to my Gobind? Why don't you speak?' Ranjit looked into her eyes and began laughing with delight. Pulling back his left hand that held the biggest prize of their lives, he unfolded the newspaper till Gobind's picture appeared on the wrinkled English daily.

'Amrita,' he began softly by steadying his voice, 'your Sat Kartar has accepted your prayers. Our son has broken

all records. He has topped the school and the state. He has scored a 100 per cent in all the subjects. The principal called to congratulate me. He wants to visit our home with his wife. Do you have some place to make them sit and some food to serve them?'

Ranjit wiped away the sweat beads that had appeared on his forehead with his hands. His face was now gleaming with joy and happiness. His eyes were filled with tears and his chest was swelled up with pride. He stood up and embraced Amrita, held her tightly for a few seconds and then whispered. 'Sat Kartar listens to you Amrita. This is a miracle. Our son has achieved what no one ever could! Seems that your Gobind actually visited our small cottage and blessed our Gobind.' He paused, letting Amrita absorb the good news and continued. 'My father often used to quote the great Saint Rahim:

> *Chah miti, chinta gayi, manua beparvah, jisko kuchh na chahiye, ve sahan ke sah.*
>
> (When desires end, worries evaporate, and the mind becomes carefree. Only he, who does not desire anything, is truly the king of kings).

'At last, I am beginning to understand the meaning of these golden words. Feels like I am the king of this universe!'

Amrita waited impatiently for Ranjit to finish speaking. And as soon as he did, she screamed with joy, hugging her husband tightly and dancing at the same time. This was

the first good news the two had received in many decades. Then, she quickly rushed to the tiny, makeshift kitchen, opened a small jar and took out some jaggery on her left palm. She put a pinch of the sweet in her husband's mouth and ate the remaining, licking with her tongue the tiniest of the particles stuck to her palm. In the same breath, she tugged at Ranjit's arm gently, guiding him to stand in front of the picture frame on the wall. Placing the newspapers at the bottom of the frame on a small platform, the couple bowed and prayed, 'Thank you, O Lord, for fulfilling our dreams, for blessing our son and for giving us so much happiness. We are ever so grateful.'

As the news began to sink in, Amrita laughed and cried at the same time. Her hands were shaking, her eyes almost popping out of their sockets as she looked closely at Gobind's picture in the papers. She couldn't read what was written but moved her palm lovingly over her son's face. She kissed the picture again and again and kept thanking the lord after every breath. After a while, she told her husband, 'Beg, borrow or steal, but please get me some money. I wish to serve the poor.'

Ranjit interrupted immediately, 'We are barely able to make two ends meet and you wish to serve the poor?'

Amrita dismissed Ranjit's comments with a flick of her head and said, 'Hands that serve are better than the hands that pray. Please arrange for some money for me by whatever means you can.'

Ranjit smiled in return. 'Sikhs never beg, Amrita. I am sure your Sat Kartar will make that arrangement too.

My bigger worry is how to receive the headmaster and his wife. We don't even have sufficient furniture to seat them properly.'

But Amrita wasn't bothered and dismissed Ranjit's worries again with a wave of her hand. 'I will make that arrangement. Leave it to me. When are they coming?'

'Tomorrow,' replied Ranjit and sank on the cot again.

4

'I can see him. Come fast!' Amrita's voice was full of thrill and excitement. She had seen Gobind. The mother in her had possibly also heard the footsteps of her son on the dusty narrow road. Ranjit rushed out, crossing Amrita midway, while she headed back indoors, only to re-emerge with a brass plate containing marigold flowers and jaggery. Women from the neighbourhood too gathered quickly. They were anticipating some news but till then weren't sure if it was going to be good or bad. As soon as they saw the shiny plate in Amrita's hands, they rushed up to her and demanded to know the reason for the celebration.

Gobind too wasn't prepared for the reception he was getting. He smiled shyly as he neared his parents. Bending low, he first touched his father's feet and was embraced immediately. Ranjit, by then, had begun to sob uncontrollably, overcome by the realization that unlike him, his only child would not become a daily wager. Amrita

showered petals while the father–son stood in embrace and garlanded Gobind as soon as Ranjit's grip loosened over her son. She wrapped him in her arms and kissed him on both cheeks. Tears welled up uncontrollably but the parents made no attempt to stop them. Their hearts were pouring out with happiness.

'Thank you, Ma, Papa,' is all Gobind could say amidst claps and cheers from the women. The proud parents led their hero indoors in the company of almost the entire neighbourhood. For the first time, their small earthen cow-dung coated veranda was filled to capacity with people. Entering the room, Gobind pushed his hand into the pocket and pulled out five Rs 100 notes. 'The headmaster gave me these and said that it was a small gift from the school.' Ranjit accepted the currency and handed it over to Amrita. 'Didn't I tell you that your Sat Kartar will take care of everything?'

Holding the crisp notes, Amrita stood in front of the picture frame on the wall, her small family on either side. As if on cue, three pairs of palms joined in prayers; the family sang the lord's praises, their moist eyes expressing gratitude. It was as if the smiling picture of Guru Gobind Singh was accepting their prayers and blessing them in return.

The news spread like wildfire, bringing the small, hitherto unknown, obscure village to life. Overnight, Gobind became their hero. Small and big newspapers, TV channels, officials and political leaders came calling. In this small village, where everyone knew everybody else, Gobind became an emblem of success and a sign of victory.

Innocent and pure at heart, the villagers cheered and lauded his achievement by pouring out in large numbers, carrying whatever gift that they could afford, filling Ranjit's small home with clothes, vegetables, hens, sheep, broom sticks, utensils, earthen pots, pigeons and even bangles. Each item indicated the profession its giver was engaged in, so none carried a name card for they all were well known by their respective professions.

Ram Dyal Sharma was aware of the financial health of Ranjit Singh's household. Breaking protocol, he arrived early with his wife, Nirmala Devi, and stood at the door receiving guests, while his wife helped Amrita with other chores. School authorities pitched up a tent right outside the house, serving everyone a glass of milk and sweets. Wearing a spotless white turban, a matching shirt and dark trousers, Ranjit stood a step behind the headmaster with his palms joined. He was overwhelmed and in complete awe of the ongoing proceedings. The school had taken over the entire function where he was expected to play the role of a chief guest. But when the village head, Bihari Lal, came calling, Ranjit stepped out of the headmaster's shadow and received him by bowing and touching his feet.

Bihari Lal embraced him in turn and then pulled out a pair of expensive looking shoes embroidered with golden thread from his bag and offered them to Ranjit. 'Your feet deserve more comfort, dear Ranjit, for your ward has put the small tracks of our village on India's map.' There was pin-drop silence as the village head continued. 'Like a mother, the soil of our beautiful village has nurtured many of my

generations. Your family has brought fame and honour to my mother. Please accept my deep and heartfelt gratitude.'

Bihari Lal's brief but strong emotional speech left even Ram Dyal overwhelmed. Despite his extensive experience, he learnt an important lesson about how one good incident could almost instantly ignite hopes, usher dreams and bring out an entire village from hibernation. Suddenly, the claps of hundreds of men engulfed the atmosphere. Scores of bare feet began stomping the dust in tune with the beats of the drums playing folk songs. Not to be left behind, the women too formed their own group. Going round in a circle, they began an impromptu jig, simultaneously singing and dancing. The entire village switched gears to be in a festive mood.

Amidst the celebrations and burst of colours, Pushpa came in through the front door. And from her shadow, a moment later, partially hidden behind her pink dupatta, appeared Meera, holding a light blue muffler. She took a step towards Gobind and extended her hands, offering him the pashmina neck wear. 'Please accept my heartiest congratulations, Gobind. I am so proud of you.' Gobind was stunned to see her, and so were Bihari Lal, Ranjit, Amrita and the villagers. The father had not expected his daughter to follow him to Ranjit's home. It was not acceptable for a girl from a high-status family to step out of her home without the consent of her parents and meet someone unknown. The expressions of disapproval on his face were overshadowed by Amrita who jumped in between the father and daughter and led Meera aside.

Holding her soft, baby-like cheeks in the cup of her palms, she looked lovingly into her eyes. 'Like Goddess Lakshmi you have come to our cottage, and I can't even offer you a suitable chair. Thank you for coming. We're so grateful to you and your family.' Meera was speechless. Being motherless, she had seldom experienced such pure, unconditional love. She gazed at the humble surroundings as Amrita escorted her into the one-room house.

The festivities soon picked up pace. Being the head of the village, Bihari Lal became the man to be for the media. Scores of cameras focused on him, giving him the same importance as they would to the village sarpanch. Feeling elated and basking in the new-found glory, he spoke like a victorious general. He glorified Gobind's hard work in his fields and lavishly praised Ranjit's sacrifices, dedication and vision in educating his son way beyond his financial capacity. When the father's turn came, he hesitated at first and then, on being prodded by the headmaster, just about managed to say few words:

> *'Na hum kiya, na kar sakenge, na kar sake sharir.*
> *Jo kiya tis Hari kiya, bhayo Kabir Kabir.'*
>
> (I did nothing, nor am I capable of doing anything. It's the Lord, who did everything, so says Kabir).

Despite all knowledge, experience, authority and position, Ram Dyal was left stumped by an illiterate, poor man's

wise comment. He nodded gently, admiring the deep-rooted meaning of the fine words uttered.

Despite the drummers going ballistic with their beats, Bihari Lal's sharp ears picked up Ranjit's response to which he added his thoughts, 'So long as we remember these golden words, dear Ranjit, we shall never go wrong in performing our karma. May God bless you and your family with many more laurels!'

While the celebrations continued, Ram Dyal signalled to Gobind and led him away from the crowd. The two walked on the narrow village road, moving away from the sound of the beats with every step. Putting his hand on Gobind's shoulders, he began in a soft tone. 'Honestly speaking, I still can't figure out how you managed to score such high marks. What are your plans from here on?'

'Sir, no institution can teach you what you learn when you're hungry and your pockets are empty. Having crossed one bridge, I wish to join the National Defence Academy (NDA). It will give my parents utmost happiness to see me wear the stars on my shoulders. I too shall get deep satisfaction by following Sardar Bhagat Singh's footsteps and becoming a soldier.'

Ram Dyal was struck by his words. He briefly stood motionless on the tracks and pondered what he had heard. Gobind's response was simple but completely unexpected. Recovering quickly, he quizzed the boy again, 'I thought you could go for higher studies and become an IAS officer. The school is willing to sponsor your studies.'

'Sir,' Gobind replied, 'I have smelt the fragrance of discipline over the past six months and enjoyed it immensely. I feel that the powerful winds of bureaucracy may corrupt and divert the purity of thoughts in my mind. The armed forces is where I belong.'

The headmaster was bowled over by the young boy's mature thoughts. 'Yesterday, when your father mentioned Sat Kartar, I was confused. But now I understand that it could only have been the heavenly blessings that have transformed you from just an ordinary boy to this new avatar. Just remember never to let small minds convince you that your dreams are too big. It is very likely that you will be tested during your journey. Keep faith and stay firm. If the lord is with you, you don't need anyone else.'

Ram Dyal stopped abruptly and then turned back. Gobind followed him. He again put his right hand on Gobind's shoulder and thoughtfully said, 'As you would be aware, every year the school takes students to Port Blair. You miss it due to financial constraints. I would like you to be part of the group this year. Of course, it will be sponsored. Now that you've decided to join the armed forces, spending quality time amongst our martyrs at what was infamously known as "kala paani" would do you a lot of good.'

Gobind nodded thoughtfully and looked towards the loudspeakers at the far end echoing the festive mood. The teacher in Ram Dyal Sharma looked happier than ever before, content that he had imparted his share of teachings to the best pupil of his school.

Once they were back home, in the crowded veranda, Gobind's eyes searched for Meera. He admired her guts to step out of the safety of her home and visit him against archaic customs and traditions. She looked beautiful, like a hand-carved porcelain doll. He rushed into the room to find Bihari Lal sitting on the cot, sipping tea from an earthen cup. Seated next to him was Meera. Ranjit and Amrita were standing close by with joined palms.

'Oh, here he comes,' said Bihari Lal. 'I was waiting for you. We should be going now.'

But as he stood up, Amrita folded her hands and pleaded. 'Let Meera be here for some more time. We will escort her home soon. Please let her be a part of the fun and enjoyment a bit longer, sir.'

Bihari Lal looked at Meera and then at his hosts. A faint, thoughtful smile appeared on his face and he nodded reluctantly, 'Okay. Gobind, please escort her home later so that you don't bother your parents. There are plenty of people out here for them to look after. But don't be late.'

He stepped out, duly escorted by Ranjit and Amrita. Gobind looked at Meera. She smiled back at him mischievously. The grin lit up her blushing face that changed many shades of pink. 'I didn't know Hira–Moti could cast such an influence on you, else I too would have spent more time with them and topped the school,' she said, and their laughter at this witty remark filled the room.

This helped to break the ice. Gobind responded, 'Thank you so much, Meera. Your coming here means so much to me. It feels like a dream that you are standing in

front of me and I am seeing you in person, in flesh and blood. I am truly grateful.'

Meera looked into his eyes and clasped his hand into hers. 'I wish to stand by you, Gobind, as your life partner. I hope the lord will listen to me. I wish to be with you in your journey ahead. I hope my prayers are answered too. I want you to know that my life is meaningless without you.'

Standing outside, the half open door, Amrita was dazed to hear Meera's words. Even in her wildest dreams, she couldn't have dreamt of such an alliance. She had to clamp her mouth shut with her hands so the sound of her heart wouldn't escape from her mouth. Then, she turned back, waited for a moment to gather her thoughts and rushed towards the veranda.

Her eyes reflected surprise, shock and fear, all at the same time. 'How can this be possible?' she murmured to herself as she stood next to Ranjit, trying to avoid the neighbours' prying eyes. Ranjit looked at her intrigued, realizing that something was amiss. He turned, looked into her eyes and walked a few steps towards her. But before he could inquire, the leather sole of his zari-embedded shoes made a creaking sound and the villagers around him began complimenting him on the new footwear. An elated Ranjit felt compelled to turn back and acknowledge their compliments.

This gave Amrita enough time to ponder the developments. Running both her hands over her head, she moved away to a corner and unconsciously nodded about a decision she had arrived at, which was that she would not

tell anyone about Meera and Gobind's affair, including her husband.

* * *

The sun was setting in the far horizon, spreading its golden rays on the green fields. Holding hands, Gobind and Meera walked on the soft, muddy track. They were mature enough to understand the huge difference in status that stood like a gigantic wall between them. Meera tried to underplay it in her efforts to calm Gobind down. 'Don't worry. Once you become a military officer, Baba will agree. He loves the army and wanted to join the forces himself. I am sure he will appreciate where his only daughter's interest lies.'

Gobind stopped and turned towards her. Holding her by her slim shoulders, he replied, 'You think so, Meera? If yes, then please wait for me. I shall come home after three years, with all the medallions on my chest. That's a promise.'

'I will,' is all Meera could say and hugged him tightly.

The setting sun took one final leap into the horizon, leaving behind a dark silhouette of the two teens merged into each other as one solitary figure under the cover of darkness.

'Why after three years, Gobind?' her words echoed in the air.

But Gobind continued to hold her tight in his embrace and didn't respond.

5

A week later, Gobind found himself sitting in front of Bihari Lal on the neatly mowed lawns. Meera saw him arrive from her balcony and rushed into the kitchen to order tea while he sat opposite the village head. Dressed in a white cotton attire, a relaxed-looking sarpanch picked up an old diary from the large round table in front and carefully flipped through the pages, one at a time. He read some portions aloud and smiled each time, recalling his younger days with a deep sigh.

'You see, Gobind, I too was very keen to join the army. But my mother did not let me do so. As a result, I could not become an officer. It's a proud moment for all of us that you have been selected by the NDA. I feel so jealous. It takes me to the time when I was desperate to be part of the military. In fact, I took Meera's late mother to the Republic Day parade several times. And had we been blessed with a boy, I would definitely have sent him to the academy.

Unfortunately, she passed away within a year of Meera's birth.' The Sarpanch paused for a few moments and scratched his head before continuing. 'I am aware of how hard you have worked to achieve your goal. Your devotion has brought honour to our village. I therefore wish to give you a befitting send off. Let your favourite Hira–Moti drive you to the end of the village. I have seen deep affection in your eyes for both the animals. I am sure it will give them immense joy too.'

Gobind didn't quite understand what to make of the offer. Bihari Lal enjoyed a status equivalent to that of a king in the village. And here he was, offering hospitality to someone who had worked on his farm as a servant. But he was in no position to question him either. He humbly bowed. 'Thanks, Baba, you're so kind.' He accepted the teacup from Pushpa, took a few sips, placed the cup on the table and said, 'Baba, could I use the restroom please?'

'Yes, why not. Pushpa will show you the way.'

Gobind stood up and walked towards the haveli. Hiding behind the pillar, Meera watched him coming towards the entrance. She ran through the alley, went past the kitchen and entered the spacious living room. Pushpa came in first, stood at the door and smilingly looked at her. 'Hey, Meera, here's your Gobind. Though, I think only Lord Krishna can keep you both together.' Pushpa exited, gently shutting the door behind her.

Meera looked at Gobind as he came closer and stood at almost touching distance. Gobind first caressed her cheeks with the back of his fingers, then her earlobes and then

gently touched her long hair. Her eyes moistened as they hugged and stayed in a tight embrace.

Meera finally broke the silence and whispered, 'Why three years? Why can't you come back after the end of each term like everybody else does? Why do you want to torture me? Why?'

Gobind held her close, her face resting on his broad chest, his chin on her head. 'For us to be together forever, I have to be worthy of your status so that Baba can accept me. Coming back every six months will make me weak. It may also create an untoward incident if we try to meet. This separation is a bridge for our togetherness. I want to achieve what no one has ever dreamt of. Just give me three years and we shall be together forever.' They stood in silence till a soft knock at the door separated the two.

Meera stepped back, went to the large sofa and picked up a small piece of rolled paper. 'Will you write to me?'

Gobind responded immediately. 'Yes, I would love to. But what if it falls into the wrong hands?'

Meera smiled in return. 'Here, send it in Pushpa's name at this address. Anyway, she gets letters from her husband.' Then she went back to pick something else and gave it to Gobind. 'This is for you. I painted it last night. But open it only once you have settled down in the academy. Just remember, Meera will only be Gobind's. No one else will ever touch her soul.' Saying this, she kissed him and ran back inside without looking back.

Gobind tucked the rolled paper inside his shirt before stepping out of the room and going back where the

Sarpanch was seated with his back to the balcony. While lifting his teacup, Gobind looked eagerly at the haveli, but there was no sign of Meera. He wanted to see her face as he exited the haveli and walked towards his new future. He sighed and stood up a few minutes later, touched Bihari Lal's feet and went towards the bullock cart. Hira–Moti shook their heads in unison in anticipation, ringing a hundred bells around their necks.

He looked back at the balcony as the cart went around the sandy track towards the exit. That's when he saw her standing on the terrace, looking at him, waving, and he smiled.

* * *

Seated uncomfortably amongst some of the elite students inside the Air India flight, Gobind kept looking at the passing clouds through the small glass window. His mother had hand-stitched his clothes and his father had pressed and packed them in a small suitcase. 'May you fly very high, my son, and test the strength of your wings. Your parents have never travelled even by train till date. Remember, you have to live your dreams as well as ours. We would like to see the world through your eyes. Ram Dyal ji had graciously sent us Rs 500 for your travel. Your school will take care of all logistics. But I want you to carry some money just in case you wish to buy something. But please don't bring anything for us. You've given us the best present any parent would ever like to be blessed with.'

Gobind closed his eyes and placed his head on the backrest. However much he tried, he could not rid his mind of his father's words that kept echoing in his ears. Many hours later, the aircraft landed on the tarmac at Port Blair. Excited like the schoolkids they were, they all began clapping. For this was their first trip to the Andaman Islands. But Gobind stayed quiet. His face was bereft of expressions and emotions.

After resting on the first night, the entourage went in buses to the Cellular Jail the next morning, accompanied by schoolteachers and an aged guide who had retired from the Indian Navy as a senior sailor. He was dressed in civilian clothes but he had proudly pinned a dozen miniature medals on the left side of his chest, while on the right side of the chest hung a small name tag that read 'Ram Singh'.

One by one, he walked the students from one prison to the other and narrated the story of each of the martyrs who had fought against the tyrannical generals of the British Raj. By the time the entourage finished the three-hour-long briefing, there was not a single dry eye. The younger lot was sobbing as if they were personally going through the trauma of the jailed freedom fighters. 'Freedom didn't come easily, dear children. Tens of thousands have been martyred for us to be free. So, think deeply before getting swayed by false political ideologies and narratives that you all build in your future.'

Soon, lunch was served and eaten by the students in pin-drop silence. Half an hour later, they all stood up and one by one made a quiet exit from the dining hall. Ram

Singh was the last to get up. His eyes weren't dry either. He could see that the sweets served to the children had remained untouched.

Back in their lodge, Gobind stepped on to the plush lawns, removed his shoes and socks and began walking barefoot on the grass. He looked deeply disturbed and emotionally unsettled. As he finished the round and neared the same place where he had left his shoes, he looked up to see the headmaster observing him closely. 'You don't look normal, son. What happened?'

Gobind looked up with moist eyes and looked down again. 'I have a question to ask. What was the need to bring students from the junior class and make them go through such heartrending stories? The trauma they have undergone will remain etched in their minds. Some of them in fact might not be able to live a normal life. Was it necessary? Perhaps there's a reason which is beyond my understanding. Can you please explain?'

Ram Dyal sat down on the nearby bench, took off his sandals and began walking on the same track that was fresh with imprints of Gobind's feet. 'I appreciate your query. And here's the explanation: Many years ago, I had an opportunity to visit Poland. A friend there took me to the gas chambers used by Hitler to kill thousands of Jews. I saw Israeli students outside, waiting for their turn to enter the chambers that have since been turned into a memorial. All kids were laughing, enjoying, celebrating their day in the sun till they entered the chambers and saw how their forefathers were tortured by the Nazis. They read the

names of thousands of innocent Jews, many related to them. They were heartbroken to hear of the ordeal each one of them had gone through. At the end of the visit, every child was shedding tears. Many lost their senses and turned hysterical. Witnessing their plight, I questioned the need to let the tiny-tots undergo such suffering. That's when I realized that it was important for the children to learn it the hard way so that they could respect the nation and become patriots in the truest sense.

'Sadly, in our country, our polity and bureaucracy no longer remember the sacrifices made by our countrymen. Freedom has been taken for granted and looting the nation is treated as an entitlement. The kids you are seeing crying today so bitterly while listening to painful history will remember what our forefathers had to suffer at the hands of the British and the traitors. Each one of them will carry a message in their minds, and that, hopefully, will help them build a productive and prosperous future. If you want gold to shine, push it through the flames!' Saying this, Ram Dyal did not wait there any longer. Slipping his feet into the sandals, he gently looked at Gobind, smiled and left.

He could make out in Gobind's expressions that the child in him was turning into a man.

6

January 1987

Over a dozen tractor trollies, loaded with children, women and farmers, both young and old, were parked on either side of the main road. Many of its passengers were holding hand-made paper flags and banners. Their eyes were focused at the long, snake-like narrow village track from where Gobind was to emerge. Their sole agenda for the day was to travel with their hero to the railway station and give him a befitting send off. For all the villagers, it was their proudest moment for no one had ever succeeded in joining the armed forces, let alone becoming a military officer.

The bullock cart had left Ranjit's haveli and was moving at a gentle pace on the track. The sarpanch held the tri-colour as if Gobind was joining the battlefield. 'God be with you, my Gobind! You've done us proud,' he said aloud as the cart began moving.

Far away on top of the white haveli stood two women. Gobind knew Meera was going through an emotional upheaval. He positioned himself at the edge of the cart and waited till the cart reached the nearest point to the haveli. He pulled open a paper sheet, unfolded it and put his hands up. 'I will miss you. Wait for me,' it read. Pushpa couldn't make out much of the text, but Meera waved back. His action, however, drew the attention of the fellow passengers who took it as a good gesture. But Amrita looked scared. She had observed the changing expressions on Ram Dyal's face. She instinctively knew that the headmaster had become aware of the connection between them.

'What if . . .' she murmured to herself looking worried.

And as soon as they saw the tall, lanky figure of the headmaster in white clothes, flanked by Ranjit Singh and Amrita and school staff, they started chanting, 'Gobind! Gobind! Gobind!' The tiny flags were being waved rapidly amidst the drumbeats. With joined palms Ranjit Singh stepped down from the bullock cart. The two beautiful animals too perhaps understood the reason for the villagers' excitement and kept shaking their heads in unison.

Gobind jumped down from the front and went up to Hira and Moti. One by one, he hugged them, his hands lovingly caressing their giant horns. The two tough-looking bulls reciprocated with equal love and in their own way let Gobind know their love for him. He drew tiny sketches on each horn for Meera to decipher. Stepping back, he looked into the eyes of the bulls and spoke to them as if they would understand his language. 'Please accept my deep gratitude,

dear Hira, Moti. I learnt many lessons in your company. It's time for me to now serve the nation.' Taking out two marigold garlands from his shoulder bag, he garlanded the beautifully decked-up bulls and touched his forehead to theirs one by one. Deeply touched by his gesture, the villagers filled the atmosphere with resounding applause.

Boarding the school bus, Gobind waved at the long caravan of trailers behind. Its passengers were now singing in celebration, making it a spectacular site. Every passerby stopped to watch the mass procession, bringing the traffic to a grinding halt. Some children even ran behind the trailers to some distance, waving and bidding farewell to their hero.

The railway station was a small, single platform junction, not too far from the village. The school administration had made a special request to the rail authorities for the train to make a brief halt and pick up its VIP passenger, a privilege that was accorded unofficially. The station was colourfully decorated with paper strings bearing Gobind's name, and standing at the entrance was none other than the station master himself, holding a bouquet of flowers. He took off his peaked cap and gave a warm hug to Gobind. The freshly polished, shining name tag hooked on to the right side of his chest read 'Kanhaiya Lal'. He escorted Gobind to the train that had arrived before time. Under the pretext of conducting some technical checks on the engine, its driver had made a brief halt at the station.

Accepting the ticket, he handed a box of home-made sweets to Gobind. 'Son, you have brought so much

honour to all of us. We are overwhelmed. Your one act has rejuvenated the entire village and rekindled hope amongst our children. This platform has never seen so many visitors in its lifetime. The entire bogey is filled with gifts that the villagers have so lovingly brought for you. Two of our employees have even taken leave just to travel with you through your journey.' Kanhaiya Lal paused, while the people close by listened to him in rapt attention.

Returning the ticket to Gobind, he continued, 'Remember son, growing old is mandatory, but growing up is optional. Make a living, not by what you get, but by what you give. Your second innings of life begins now. It might be a little tough, but it is entirely up to you to make it a masterpiece. You're our hope, our flag bearer. Please stay connected for we all shall be praying for your safety and success. May God be with you.' That the station master's brief speech had made a lasting impression was visible in most people's expressions.

Gobind too was deeply touched by the emotion-filled words of advice. He bowed to touch the old man's feet and felt two hands on top of his turban, blessing him in return. The station master also chanted Bhagavad Gita *slokas*, invoking the gods to bless Gobind. The engine driver let off a loud whistle. Dressed in a smart white attire, the guard waved the green flag. The big metallic wheels screeched into action, setting into motion all the attached bogeys. Gobind looked at his mother. Tears rolled out of her eyes uncontrollably as if her only son was going to the battlefield. He hurriedly hugged her. 'I shall miss you, Ma,' he managed to utter.

Amrita stroked Gobind's back and kissed him on his forehead. Then, she looked up into her son's eyes and spoke softly. 'It's just that I am not used to not seeing you back home every day, Gobind. I have to learn that my little bird has grown up and is flying away to build his own nest. I have one request to make.' Gobind stepped back, surprised. He looked into her eyes and pleaded. 'Please tell me Ma. Just direct me.'

Amrita made no attempt to wipe off the tears that were rolling down in a steady stream. Her hands touched his face, and she spoke in a tone that Gobind had never heard before. She looked emotional yet firm and commanding. She looked deep into his eyes, touching his very soul. 'It is quite possible, Gobind, that in the line of your duty, you might face a challenging situation, a conflict or a war,' she began. 'Face it head on. Ensure that you receive no wound on your back. You owe it to our gurus who taught us to never surrender. May the lord protect you, always.' Completing her sentence, she gently wiped her face with a *chunni* and put her hands on his head. Far from any regret in her voice, she actually felt relieved to have done her duty.

Gobind was taken aback. He had not expected his mother to make such a strong statement. A few women standing close by hurriedly put their hands over their mouths. Their eyes were widened in shock, realizing the far-reaching meaning of Amrita's directive to her only son. Many turned their faces towards each other with expressions of disbelief, checking if what they had heard was indeed correct. As thin as a frail leaf, Amrita stood

firmly, making sure that her son had understood her command.

The second long whistle of the engine broke the hushed silence. 'I will Ma,' he responded softly and turned towards his father, hurriedly hugging him before rushing into the compartment. His eyes were still fixed on his mother amidst a hundred waving hands and chants of '*Jai Sri Ram*' and '*Jo bole so nihal*'. The whistling engine began rolling the giant wheels. 'May god be with you,' shouted the headmaster, as the train picked up speed.

Standing at the door, Gobind looked at the sea of humans on the platform. His parents stood in front, holding on to each other with one hand and waving with the other till the train was out of sight. Gobind stepped back, shut the door and looked at the compartment that was filled with all kinds of gifts. Stretching his hand, he pulled out a small cage that had two beautiful green parrots in it. He was aware of the pure hearts of his village folks, but he also knew that caged birds weren't going with him to the academy.

A faint smile broke on his sad face. Turning around, he opened the compartment door and held the cage close to his eyes. The parrots looked back, as if expecting sermons from their new master. 'You both are like my Hira–Moti. Please fly high into the sky and request the lord up there to take care of my Meera.' With that, he flung open the door. There was a sudden gush of wind on his face. He unlocked the cage and opened the tiny door. The two parrots looked back at their master but made no attempt to fly out. Gobind

nudged them gently till one of them stepped forward. The second one followed. With one long leap, the two flew into the open sky, their wings flapping as rapidly as they could. Their shrieks while flying out were filled with the joy of freedom that was their birthright but had been taken away by greedy humans.

Before returning to his seat, he stood there for a few minutes, watching them rest on the branches of trees they'd landed on. The two co-passengers sitting in front smiled at him, carefully observing his every move. 'My name is Ram,' began one of them. 'And he's Kishan. We both work in the railways. What you achieved was unthinkable till yesterday. But now, we too have begun dreaming, thus this journey with you. So please help us, advise us and talk to us about it.'

Gobind managed to nod somehow and held their hands. But his mind and heart were completely filled with thoughts of Meera. He hurriedly stood up and pulled out the black trunk from beneath the seat. Unlocking it, he pulled out the neatly rolled paper and was about to open it when he recalled Meera's words. 'Please open it only after reaching the academy.' He smiled at the thought, kissed the roll, gently placed it back in the trunk and locked it before pushing it back under the seat. Confused, the two young men looked at each other and then at him but stayed quiet. Gobind took the opposite bunk and began chatting with them.

* * *

Khadki, a small, quiet and mostly deserted railway station near the National Defence Academy in Khadakwasla, Pune, had sprung to life to receive its new recruits. Smartly dressed jawans in crisp, olive-green khakis were busy unfolding a long row of tables and marking them in alphabetical order. Each long table was manned by an instructor and a few helpers to register the new arrivals from different parts of the country. As the whistling engine made its way towards the platform, the help desks prepared to move into action. Almost the entire train was full of teenagers who were soon to be addressed as cadets for the next three years. They disembarked one by one, and, as expected, looked quite lost.

Everyone, without exception, could be seen pulling out a black steel trunk from their respective bogies that measured exactly 100, 55 and 25 centimetres in length, breadth and height, respectively, designed to fit under the cots in their rooms at the academy. Each trunk bore the name of its owner. Some had even added their father's names and that of their villages. Their attire too highlighted the culture and the city they'd came from. This spectacular site drew a lot of attention from the local passengers who stood watching this fancy-dress ceremony on display.

Amongst the first ones to disembark and reach the reception desk was a dark complexioned, tall and slim teenager. He was wearing a loosely wrapped lungi with a white cotton shirt. He dragged the black trunk and stood in front of the subedar, his black hair shining brightly in the sun. Subedar Bhawani Singh was a seasoned, battle-

hardened soldier. He looked at the youngster closely, smiled under his mustache, extended his hand and shook it gently, 'What's your name, young man?'

'Muthuswami. RMPBS Muthuswami, saab. I am from Kamputhoori district, Mudrass,' he said in a heavy accent.

'You are welcome, son. Please go and sit in bus number 1. Leave the trunk here. It will be handed over to you at the academy.'

Muthu's eyes and ears were focused on the subedar's face, trying to grasp every alphabet being uttered by the smartly dressed instructor, while trying to read the shiny name tag on his chest. The subedar, in the meanwhile, picked up a paper towel from the desk and wiped off the oil from his hand and sniffed his palms. 'How much coconut oil have you applied, Muthu?'

Muthu did not respond but looked in the direction of Bhawani Singh's finger that was pointing towards the bus parked outside the station.

Moving back, he acknowledged the signal he had been given and responded in his accented English, 'Yuss saab,' and hurriedly walked away.

The subedar's eyes followed him briefly and then turned towards the next teenager who had by then reached the front desk.

Gobind waited for his turn but intently listened to the subedar's instructions to the cadets in front. As he inched towards the desk, the aura of military life, its systematic working style, discipline and work culture began making inroads into his mindset. He observed how each

workstation was meticulously manned and attended to to ensure minimum waiting time for the cadets. Soon, it was his turn. Bhawani Singh looked hard into Gobind's eyes and his turban. He then bent his head just a little and glanced at the trunk before asking confidently, 'You are Gobind from Punjab?'

'I am Gobind from Patna, Bihar, saab,' Gobind responded with a straight face.

Caught on the wrong foot, the Subedar's eyes widened. He bent his head again to take a closer look at the steel trunk. The handwritten white paint on the black box read, 'Gobind Singh, Patna Sahib, Bihar.'

A big smile spread on his face. 'Pleasure to meet you. Welcome to your new home. Er, why have you written "Sahib" after Patna on your trunk?'

Gobind shook the hand and looked at his trunk for a moment. 'Because my guru was born in Patna. Therefore, it's a holy city for me.'

The subedar's eyes widened. 'Oh, okay. Please board bus number 3. I will be your drill instructor for the next three years.'

Gobind did not quite understand what to make of the subedar's words. Despite the firmness in his command, Bhawani Singh's voice carried distinct politeness. Handing over his trunk to the waiting helper, he followed the line of cadets heading towards the exit. After walking a few steps, he turned his head to find the subedar too looking in his direction. The look on his face showed that he was embarrassed by his wrong guess.

Gobind nodded his head slightly at him and then turned towards the waiting bus and exited through the big, old and dilapidated wooden gate at the Khadki station. Without introducing himself to the other cadets seated in the bus, he took the first window seat diagonally opposite the driver's. Being a small station, there wasn't much hustle and bustle around. The staring passengers too had gone their own way. Calmness prevailed outside the station. He looked around as much as he could. Not too far away was a huge tree, on the branch of which sat two parrots. Gobind's eyes lit up. 'Hira–Moti!' he exclaimed with joy, but soon realized his mistake. Resting his head on the backrest, his mind drifted back to his mother's words. 'Receive no wound on your back . . .' Closing his eyes, he spoke softly, 'I won't, Ma, I promise.'

The buses sped on the broken Pune roads, which were flanked by illegal construction, make-shift kiosks and haphazardly planned colonies. Manoeuvring the hurdles and potholes, the buses went past the maze of chaos as if they were under the command of fighter pilots. An hour later, the fleet entered the tall, solid steel gates and crossed the reddish-pink Kota stone pillars of India's premier military academy, the NDA. The whole landscape changed dramatically, as if a magic wand had been waved over it! Unplanned roadside development gave way to a lush green cover that was spread till the far horizon under the clear blue skies. Everything looked neat and clean, and methodically planned.

Gobind took in the scenery. There were thick jungles all around that were surrounded by tall hills. One could

even hear the occasional big cat roar. A tall pink-stone edifice within a valley, the grand structure of the academy stood testimony to the country's rich heritage and glory. To Gobind, it appeared like a big canvas had been painted by heavenly bodies in a bright lush green colour, with a touch of royal architecture. It had been protected and maintained with utmost dedication and devotion, and its military officers, some of the finest in the country, were a testimony to the training it gave.

As the caravan of buses moved, the driver of the leading bus suddenly hit the brakes, bringing all the buses behind to a screeching halt. Gobind stood up from his seat and balanced himself by holding the hand rest. What he saw in front was spectacular, to say the least, and would be etched in his mind for times to come. In front of them, a short distance away, a large passel of boars was scampering across the road in a frenzy. Emerging from somewhere in the dense green cover, the panic-stricken wild pigs jumped upon the roads in droves. They were making strange noises. Then, one by one, they leapt into the safety of the jungle on the other side in a flash.

Gobind had never seen a boar in his life before. One look at the driver's unimpressed, calm face told him that it was routine business at the NDA. But what transpired thereafter took even the driver by complete surprise. The boars had barely crossed the road when two fully grown leopards landed bang in the centre of the concrete track. The predators that had come chasing the boars were visibly startled and stood for a brief moment looking at the boars

as they vanished into the jungle in quick succession. The wild cats then looked at each other, and within a fraction of a second, took one long leap into the jungle they had come from, abandoning the hunt. There was a resounding round of applause by the cadets. It became clear to Gobind that human presence was interfering with the natural habitat of wildlife. However, not a single human being except Gobind had registered that.

It took some time before the buses began their movement towards the academy. The driver in the first bus had slowed the speed, possibly hoping to see some more action. He had seen boars on numerous occasions and was also aware of the presence of big cats in the dense jungle. But in his long service at the NDA, he had never come across such vicious-looking wild cats at such close quarters. Driving carefully, he brought the bus to a halt at the large, cemented parade ground. He waited for a brief moment, looked around cautiously before jumping out of the bus. Then, he walked to the other side and opened the passenger door, gesturing to the cadets to disembark. Beneath his peak cap, reflecting the bright sun rays, were sweat drops that shone brightly. Wiping them off with his bare hands, he murmured to himself, 'Damn. I hope I am not going to be hunted like a pig by those big cats.'

The cadets disembarked and assembled on the parade ground for allotment of squadrons. Like a well-rehearsed drill, the instructors marched in. The seniormost among them stepped out and stood in front of the assembled teenagers. In his left hand was a blue-coloured cardboard

folder, which he opened as if carrying out a precision task: his head bending just enough, his back ramrod straight and his hands holding on to the file gently. In front of him, he could see an unkempt lot of teenagers. Without reacting to their casual, unmilitary behaviour, he began his address, 'Welcome to the NDA. Your squadron will be your address at the NDA for the next three years. You're expected to build pillars for yourself that will serve you in the future. The academy will also be an emblem of recognition for the rest of your life. If you do well, your name will get etched in history books and cherished for generations to come. So do well and give your best. May god be with you.'

Then, he scanned the large crowd in front of him. There was a hushed silence. Scores of innocent, young and hopeful faces waited expectantly for what was to come next. The calm but strong aura of the officer, his elegant dress, his commanding presence were enough to keep them still. Perhaps the instructor too expected that effect. Without displaying any emotions, he began announcing the name and squadron of each cadet. Not too far away, the trucks carrying the trunks from the station lined up in a formation. Glancing at the trucks, he continued. 'Buses will drop you outside your respective squadrons. Please carry your luggage to your allotted cabins and settle down. You're expected to assemble outside the cadet's mess for lunch within sixty minutes. Any questions?'

The directive from the instructor was loud and clear, leaving no scope for doubts. But Muthu wasn't clear. Holding one end of his lungi between the fingers of his

left hand's, he raised his other arm in an artistic manner and walked past the row of cadets towards the podium. The instructor looked at him closely. His face broke into a controlled smile. 'Any questions?' he demanded in a crisp voice. Muthu looked left, right and then back at the instructor. Hesitatingly, he spoke, 'But saab, my trunk is very, very heavy. Where can I get a coolie?'

The instructor smiled broadly while his colleagues standing behind him started laughing, breaking the stern expressions they were used to carrying all the time. 'Please carry the trunk on your head and run. You have one hour to settle down. Be present at the dining hall. If you are late, you will miss lunch! Disperse!' Instinctively, the cadets ran towards the parked vehicles and to their respective squadrons thereon. Muthu too understood that he was not going to get any help and if he didn't hurry, he would have to skip his lunch too.

Not too far away, the stewards at the dining hall began setting the long tables with crockery and cutlery.

Still smiling, the head instructor went past his colleagues and gestured to a small group of civilians who too were enjoying the ongoing drama. One of them rushed to the instructor and waited for his command. 'Zero cut, everyone. I want no hair on their heads.' The barber smiled and rushed back to his group. They were all accustomed to the ritual and needed no briefing. So, as soon as the instructors departed, the barbers too dispersed towards the squadron buildings and began setting up their mobile hair-cutting saloon. Holding the long shaving blades by

their wooden handles, they began rubbing them on coarse stones, sharpening the edges for the impending sacrifice of hair from across the country.

After a brief lull, the NDA building was abuzz with activity again.

At the dining table, the sighting of the two leopards was the hot topic of discussion. By the time lunch got over, the hush-hush discussion had travelled from one end of the huge dining hall to the other, and like it happens in a game of Chinese whispers, the size of the two leopards had grown over 10 feet! Each cadet used his own cinemascope version to describe the animals. Despite having witnessed the incident from close quarters, Gobind stayed calm and paid little attention to the gossip. His mind was focused on the alphabet 'A' that was etched on top of the entrance of the building he had entered to deposit his luggage. 'Alpha Squadron' was going to be the suffix to his name for times to come.

He had, by then, also learnt that Subedar Bhawani Singh was the toughest drill instructor. While most cadets got their hair cut, Gobind being a Sikh had plenty of time to go around the hall, admiring the glittering trophies, memoirs and photo frames of battle heroes. His mother's words, 'receive no wound on your back . . .', kept echoing in his mind as he read the names of the war heroes on the polished wood-panelled walls. An hour later, he was back in his room.

Pulling the trunk from beneath his bed, he opened the lid and carefully unwrapped the neatly rolled paper.

It turned out to be a painting in bright watercolours. He then spread it on the table and looked at it intently. Two bullocks tied to a bullock cart stood on a deserted track. Since their horns matched those of Hira–Moti's, he assumed it was them. Standing in front of the of the cart was Meera, wearing a red silk scarf and holding a garland in her hands. She was staring into the distant horizon, waiting for her Gobind. At the bottom right corner a short note was inscribed, 'I am tying knots on my red silk scarf, my beloved. I am waiting for you, remembering you every fleeting moment. Yours forever, Meera.'

Gobind admired the painting for a long time. She had opened her heart in those beautifully crafted words. He hummed the lyrics in the same tone in which Meera had sung them so often, even though he wasn't sure if her father would ever agree to such a match. He could feel her pain as three years were going to be a long separation. Placing the painting back in the trunk, he lay down on the bed. And soon as he did, his heart raced him back to the haveli. He found himself holding Meera in a tight embrace. This made him restless. He tossed and turned, thinking of ways to connect with her. The exhaustion had its desired effect. Before long, Gobind was fast asleep.

7

Inter-squadron rivalry was an accepted feature in most military establishments. And the NDA wasn't an exception. Each commander ensured that his squadron turned out with the best possible results. In Gobind, Subedar Bhawani Singh had found someone who had the potential of bringing home the parade and drill trophy and someone who could command the final passing out parade. He made him go through extra hardships if he made the slightest error. As a result, the many dusty layers on the precious but raw diamond that Gobind was began clearing, leaving behind a gem that shone through its many facets.

Before going to bed each night, Gobind made it a routine to pen down his daily activities, which, by the end of the week, would run into a few pages. Every Sunday, he mailed them home in the form of a letter. Even though his parents couldn't read, he was confident that his school headmaster would make suitable arrangements for his

letters to be read. On his part, Ram Dyal Sharma made it a point to visit Ranjit Singh's home every week and read the letters out loud as if reading a newspaper. Ranjit's veranda soon became a weekend tea hub for the villagers. Ranjit and Amrita swelled with pride when anyone addressed Gobind as the 'Son of Bihar'. Gobind also never missed writing to Meera and anxiously waited to hear from her. Pushpa became a safe conduit, and an efficient and reliable postman.

By the end of the first term, it became clear to everyone in the academy that Gobind was a man on a mission. Meera's letters always proved to be an energy booster, raising his performance by many notches. Be it cross country or the equestrian, he outshone everyone with ease. Be it demanding marching drills on the parade ground, lectures by professors, evening sports or night-time studies, he was never found lacking. He faced every obstacle head on and took up challenging assignments with deep determination, while maintaining a calm and composed exterior. His drill instructor, however, soon found out about the layers of pain he hid beneath his innocent, smiling face. Muthuswami became his soulmate and was often seen in his company, possibly because both had come from similar humble backgrounds.

If there was one area that bothered Gobind immensely, it was swimming. And he did poorly in the first term. It was compulsory for every cadet to pass the test as was to jump from a 10-metre board. The penalty on not being able to do it was severe and relegation was mandatory, which meant you were held back and had to repeat the term.

During the second term, one Sunday morning, the entire Alpha squadron was asked to report at the pool. Their first task was to jump from a 5-metre board and swim the full length of the pool. There were many who dreaded the very look of the deep blue water from that height and wondered how they would jump. Being a naval cadet, it was even more important for Gobind to qualify. Sharp at 0600 hrs, the tests commenced. At the blow of the whistle, the cadets, in batches of six, trooped up the ladder to the 5-metre board and jumped into the pool in quick succession. It was all going smoothly, like a well-oiled machine.

However, like all battle plans, there were glitches. Some cadets refused to jump. It took a lot of cajoling and threats to make them take the leap. Often, the instructor had to climb up the ladder and literally push the cadets off from the diving board. The inordinate delay resulted in exhausting the allotted pool time for the cadets. Soon, the officers and their families began to arrive. And amongst them was Tina Singh, the beautiful daughter of the commandant. Her presence in a two-piece tight-fit swimsuit encouraged the remaining cadets to get over their fear and jump off the board just to show off their manliness. But Gobind simply refused to bite the bait. The angry instructor climbed up the ladder to push him down, but Gobind used the side pole to do a monkey climb down.

This drama went on as if it were some sort of catch-me-if-you-can game. The two could not meet at a common ground, quite literally, leaving the assembled crowd in a fit

of laughter. The divisional officer's whistle too had lost its relevance and hung loosely around his neck. Embarrassed, the training officer looked helplessly at the crowd that was enjoying Gobind's monkey tricks. 'Sir, let me try and make him jump,' volunteered Tina Singh and began climbing the ladder. Dumbfounded, the instructor sheepishly stepped aside. She reached the top wearing a big smile and offered her hand to Gobind. Then holding him by his arm, she sweet talked him into walking with her, hand in hand, till the edge of the board. A hundred jealous eyes watched the drama unfold. When they reached the edge, Gobind slid his hands to her waist, and without giving her any warning, gave her a gentle push. Before Tina could react and regain balance, she fell from the 5-metre board flat into the pool, splashing water on the onlookers. Filled with anger, she stepped out and wrapped herself with a large towel.

By then, the commandant too had arrived. Fuming in anger, he ordered the training officer to bring Gobind down the ladder. Stepping down, he came running and stood in front of the commandant to face his wrath. 'I am giving you one last opportunity. Are you going to jump?' he asked aloud.

'Yes Sir!' Gobind answered in a loud parade-ground voice.

'Then, don't waste any more time and complete the drill,' shouted back the commandant.

Gobind went back to the ladder and quickly climbed up the 5-metre board. Facing the commandant, he said, 'Sir, can I jump from the10-metre board instead?'

'Why not? That's the spirit I like to see. Now, show me that you can do it, and your misbehaviour shall be forgiven,' beamed the commandant with a broad satisfied grin. A shocked audience counted each step. Gobind climbed slowly to reach the 10 m height. He went to the middle of the platform and stood at attention for almost a minute. His muscular, perfectly shaped body with prominent biceps, pectoral muscles and abs looked impressive and spectacular. He was like Adonis, waiting for the inevitable. Standing down not too far away, Tina huddled on the side of the pool like a wet otter, looking at Gobind with doleful eyes. The commandant was probably hyper ventilating. There was pin drop silence. All eyes turned to look up, some lips moving in prayers as a refusal now would mean relegation.

Slowly, Gobind took three steps and went to the very edge. He took another few deep breaths, shook his shoulders to relax, his eyes focused on the distant horizon. Very slowly, in perfect slow motion, he did a handstand at the edge of the 10-metre board. He stayed like this for another half minute, perfectly still, head craned backwards, his toes pointing towards the sky.

All of a sudden, he pushed his body up with his hands and forward like a Polaris missile from a submarine. For a second or two, he stretched his hands out, in an inverted crucifix position, body stiff and toes pointing straight at the sky. As the gravity took hold, he rolled himself into a ball, clasping his knees with both hands, chin tucked into his chest, somersaulting backwards once . . . twice . . . thrice. As he approached the water, his body uncoiled, hands

above his head and his back ramrod straight. He dived perfectly, with hardly a splash. In diving terms, it was an inverted triple somersault, with a pike value of 4.9, a most difficult one, executed like an Olympian diver.

There was absolute silence. One couldn't hear anyone breathing. The crowd held its breath waiting for Gobind to surface from the deep end. Everyone waited and waited, but there was no sign of him. Suddenly, there was a splash at the opposite end of the pool—the shallow end. Gobind pulled himself out of the water like a dolphin.

Amidst applause and cheer came a loud order, 'Cadet, come here.' The commandant was shouting louder than the others. Everyone was clapping, applauding and cheering. Tina was the loudest. But without acknowledging or even reporting to the commandant, Gobind ran like a hare in his swimming trunks. He sped to the gym, behind the QM fort and kept running as if the devil were after him. He went back to the Alpha Squadron and hid in the tearoom behind the parapet for the next two hours.

The next morning, he was marched up to the commandant, who got up from his chair to shake his hands but awarded him fourteen days' restriction for shirking. 'Swimming tests had to be cancelled due to your drama at the pool. Explain this to me,' demanded the commandant, 'when did you learn swimming? Your record shows that you are not a swimmer. More importantly, when did you learn diving?'

'Sir,' explained Gobind, 'I began training in the pool every day, one hour prior to the official opening of the pool

and also did extensive training during the first term break in Pune.'

'Then why did you create so much ruckus at the pool?' The commandant was now trying not to smile.

Gobind smiled back. 'Sir, I didn't know you had arrived.'

'Get lost! If I hear you doing another prank, I won't hesitate to relegate you.' The commandant paused briefly, smiled and continued in a polite tone, 'But honestly, Gobind, I am impressed. I admire your spirit. You're a gem, a rare one at that. Well done. Please join me for tea at my residence during the coming weekend. Your divisional officer will fine tune the schedule.' The sudden change in tone followed by an invitation shook up Gobind. He looked at his boss, who almost roared again. 'Now scram!' Only this time, there was deep affection in his voice. A daily wager's son was climbing up the military leadership ladder at a rapid pace, and he felt proud to see the young man do so successfully. Gobind saluted smartly, turned towards the door and marched out of the spacious room.

Gobind's friendly, low-profile and positive attitude had also made him the hero of his squadron and the cynosure of all eyes. It became clear to the leadership at the NDA that Gobind was a man on a mission with a will power to match. Cadets from other squadrons had also become aware of the 'magic letters' that the postman delivered every week without fail. If the whisper campaign was to be believed, these letters were solely responsible for Gobind's record-breaking performances. By the end of the first term, he had

won top honours in equestrian and cross-country events and studies. Above all, he was rated best in drill, which kept him in the limelight throughout. Swimming, once the weakest link in his profile till the first term, had turned out to be his strongest point at the academy, so much so that each time he entered the pool, he was asked to jump from the 10-metre board.

Tina's soft corner for Gobind too became an open secret. The more he kept away from the pool to avoid controversies, the more murmurs spread of their growing relationship. It was a blessing in disguise for him that by the time he finished his second term, Tina had to leave the NDA for higher studies abroad.

At the NDA, after every six months, the sixth term cadets pass out after the ceremonial parade. In the final term, all the cadets march to the famous Khetarpal Square. While cadets from the first to the fifth term march past the QM Fort, the final-term cadets march past the quarterdeck in their final parade. After each term break, much against his father's wishes, Gobind stayed back in Pune at a course mate's home. Aware of her son's affair with Meera, Amrita refrained from showing a keenness for Gobind to return home for vacations. She was well aware of the village head Bihari Lal's possessiveness when it came to Meera and feared for the safety of her only child. She was sure that the panchayat head would never tolerate a daily wager's son to be linked to his only daughter, who lived like a princess in the palatial haveli. Honour killing was a common and widely prevalent custom in rural India, and she did not

want Gobind to get caught in the crossfire. She somehow persuaded her husband to let their son stay in Pune without sharing the actual reason with him.

By the time Gobind reached the sixth and final term, he had left his stamp of authority on every competition he had participated in. His all-round superlative performances across the board had made him an undisputed choice as the parade commander and also an automatic choice for the coveted President's gold medal.

Both Ranjit and Amrita were invited by the commandant to attend the passing-out ceremony in December 1989. Accompanied by Ram Dyal, the parents arrived at the academy well in time and were awestruck to see the vast and immaculately maintained academy. Being parents of a cadet who was to command the parade and also receive a gold medal from the army chief, they were accommodated in the VIP enclosure to witness the final passing-out parade. Ranjit and Amrita had stepped out of Patna for the first time and looked completely mesmerized by the military establishment and the clockwork precision with which it functioned. Neat, clean and dressed up like a bride, the NDA was at its attractive best. Hundreds of cadets marching together in their khakis on the vast grounds was a sight they couldn't take their eyes off, and seeing their son commanding the parade made it nearly impossible for them to control their emotions.

Sitting in the fourth row in the special enclosure, Amrita's eyes were glued to only one spot. Standing well ahead of the sea of smartly turned-out cadets was her son,

shouting marching orders. At each command, the entire contingent moved like an automatic, well-oiled machine with such precision that it left the spectators in complete awe. Emotionally overwhelmed, deeply excited and nearly out of her breath, Amrita found it difficult to remain seated. At the slightest action in the drill, she would stand up and clap out loud. The people seated nearby felt awkward and even commented softly, but she paid no attention and continued to cheer her son. Holding the edges of her pallu in her frail hands, she stayed glued to her spot and eagerly waited for Gobind to receive the medallion. As soon as the chief guest clasped the President's gold medal on Gobind's chest, the dam of her emotions broke open. Exhilarated, she shook from head to toe, her entire body expressing the joys that her soul had been praying for since many years. Tears flowed uncontrollably from her eyes while she clapped and jumped. 'Look, he is my son, my Gobind. He is my Gobind . . . my Gobind,' she said loudly and repeatedly. Her words echoed in the VIP enclosure, taking the large gathering by complete surprise.

People sitting close by began observing her carefully. She was dressed in a simple cotton saree and her grey hair was tied at the back of her head in a bun. Her frail body and lack of jewellery showcased her humble background. But what moved people the most were her free-flowing tears of joy. A mother's true expressions of love for her child were breaking all barriers and casting a deep impression on the audience witnessing the proceedings. The assembled guests saw in her a parent who had made enormous sacrifices

just to see her son stand tall and proud and be bestowed with top honours. An elderly retired army general sitting nearby stood up and joined her in clapping. And, soon, the entire VIP enclosure broke out in a thunderous applause. Their smiles, expression and applause didn't seem to reach Amrita's ears. She paid little attention to the commotion her actions were causing. Nor did she make any attempt to wipe off the tears that were flowing down her cheeks. She remained in ecstasy and her lips repeatedly kept murmuring, 'My Gobind. He's my Gobind; look, he's my Gobind.'

It didn't take much time for the chief guest to appreciate the reason behind her outburst. Breaking protocol, he walked to where she stood. All the guests stood up again to see the army chief coming towards them. Officers in uniform saluted the general, while the civilian guests bowed gently. Acknowledging their gesture by saluting in return, the chief walked past the front rows and stood in front of Amrita. He folded his hands as the flabbergasted Amrita twisted the edges of her saree between her thin fingers. The general smiled gently, helping her ease up before speaking softly, 'Ma'am, your joys, your emotions and the enormous pain hidden therein have taken me down memory lane. It reminds me of my mother who made many sacrifices to ensure that I achieved my goals. I am so proud to see what your son has gifted you today. Please accept my heartiest congratulations.' The army chief saluted her again and turned back, leaving an overwhelmed Amrita looking tearfully at him. Moved by the chief guest's unprecedented gesture, the crowd burst into an applause yet again.

After the spectacular drill and ceremonies, the young parade commander marched past the quarterdeck in slow steps, marking the end of the passing-out parade and found his drill instructor, Subedar Bhawani Singh. Standing in attention, the drill instructor stamped his foot hard on the ground while simultaneously touching his hand to his brow, completing what could be termed as a smart army salute. Gobind acknowledged and continued marching forward till he reached the designated spot. The passing-out parade drill for Gobind was done. Alpha Squadron had won the most-coveted parade and drill trophy, and Gobind's name was etched in the history books of the NDA forever. He had accomplished his dream and that of his drill instructor's. He stopped at the far end post and turned right.

He walked up to Bhawani Singh and stood in front of him. His chest was now proudly displaying the gold medal, and his heart was filled with pride for having achieved the highest honour. 'Thank you, saab. I am so grateful to you. I shall never forget you for the rest of my life,' he managed to say before bending to touch his instructor's feet.

Bhawani was taken aback by his action. Holding Gobind's shoulders with his strong arms, he said, 'Please don't do this. You're now an officer. I just did my duty, sir. It was the fire in you that propelled you all the way. You've a great future ahead. May god be with you.' But even the tough subedar within him couldn't stop him from taking Gobind in a tight embrace. 'I am proud of you, son, very proud of you. Thank you for giving me so much respect.'

After the ceremony, the cadets returned to the parade ground to celebrate the successful completion of their three-year training. Gobind was mobbed and tossed up in air by his squadron cadets amidst applause from a host of others. From the veranda of a humble cottage in Patna, the festivities had travelled a long way to rekindle abundant happiness and hopes in the hearts of Amrita and Ranjit. Standing a short distance away in the company of a beaming Ram Dyal and Bhawani Singh, they looked at their only child, now grown up into a tall and handsome young man, enjoying his day in the sun. When Bhawani Singh offered them a tour of the academy, they readily agreed, except for Amrita. She had some news to break to her son.

Half an hour later, mother and son were sitting next to each other in a large room. Gobind looked into her eyes and immediately sensed that she had something serious to convey. He inquired, 'Is something bothering you, Ma? Please share it with me.' Amrita had planned to take her time in revealing the information, but when her son asked, she felt as if she'd been caught. Amrita looked startled while Gobind continued. 'I had noticed this earlier too, but I assumed it was an error in my judgement. But now I am quite certain that you're hiding something. I am eager to know. Please tell me.'

Amrita put her hands on Gobind's cheeks, caressed them gently and began in a soft, emotional voice, 'My child, you have now become a military officer. There will be many instances when you'll have to just bow down before destiny. We as parents will always give you our love. But we cannot

give you the high status that is equally important.' She paused and looked at Gobind who, by then, was looking worried. Amrita continued, 'So what I am sharing with you is not going to be easy. But you'll have to accept it as a fait accompli.' Gobind stayed calm and waited for his mother to let out the secret. She spoke again, 'Bihari Lal has fixed Meera's marriage with the son of the MLA of Purnia.' She paused after this and looked carefully at her son's face and instantly realized the extent of hurt that he was absorbing without giving away much.

Recovering slowly, he looked up to his mother's face and said, 'But why are you telling me this?'

'Because I know you both love each other.'

Shocked upon hearing his mother's words, Gobind stood up. Amrit expected that and continued. 'The headmaster tried to intervene and even spoke to Bihari Lal ji. But he rudely brushed it aside citing the huge status difference between our families.'

'Ma,' Gobind began in almost a whisper, 'Did Meera talk to you?'

'No, she did not. I was outside the door when Meera expressed her desire to be your life partner. I have seen deep love for you in her eyes. I couldn't share this with anyone, not even your father, till I learnt about the news of her marriage being fixed. I wanted you to be prepared with this development before you returned to the village.'

Gobind sat down again and bent his head as if he was immersed in deep thoughts. Without looking up, he softly muttered, 'I am not going back, Ma. It will hurt me

even more. I will not be able to face Meera. I am going to Bombay.'

Amrita stood up and held her son in a tight embrace. 'I know, Gobind, what you're going through. Even in this hour of celebration, I wanted you to be aware of the harsh reality.' Amrita's voice was sombre but in control.

The sound of the approaching metallic boots on the cemented floor in a perfect rhythm alerted the mother and son. They looked up to see Subedar Bhawani Singh walking into the room. Standing at the door were Ranjit and Ram Dyal, listening intently to their conversation. Gobind took a step back and looked at the drill instructor with moist eyes.

Bhawani put his hand on his shoulders and gently smiled. 'Son, there's something that you must understand. Soldiers and sacrifices always go hand in hand. Unlike the civilian world out there, we don't have the luxury of time to look back. Indeed, I am sad to hear what you have gone through at this young age. But you'll need to learn to keep your feelings within so that no one can tell by your expressions. Just remember, you'll never meet a strong person with an easy past.'

8

All the leading newspapers in Patna flashed pictures of Gobind receiving the President's gold medal from the army chief. The headline in one of the newspapers read: 'Son of Bihar Emerges as Top Military Hero'. Another prominent English daily's frontpage headline stated: 'Patna Boy Conquers Military Academy'.

On her routine visit to the bazar, Pushpa saw Gobind's pictures in the newspapers at the kirana shop. She hurriedly grabbed all the papers and scanned the news items in each. Folding them inside out lest someone at the haveli noticed its contents, she stacked them neatly inside her grocery bag, hailed a rickshaw and exited the market without completing her shopping. Fifteen minutes later, she was climbing the stairs holding the vegetable bag firmly in her right hand, clinging on to the edges of her saree with the other. She knocked at Meera's door while pushing it open. A startled Meera looked up. But before she could demand

an explanation, Pushpa shut the door, ran to her and pulled out the papers.

Handing them over to her, she took deep breaths and said in a conspiratorial whisper, 'Please open them.' Then, without waiting for her response, she picked up her bag and ran to the door and exited, shutting the door behind her. Meera followed her till the door and locked it from inside and then ran to her bed. Spreading the papers one by one on the white bed sheet, she looked at the pictures carefully. Dressed in smart khakis and wearing the shining medallion on his chest was indeed her very own Gobind—a broad smile on his bearded face. Looking carefully, she ran her finger on Gobind's quote, 'I owe this to an angel who inspired me to dream the impossible dream.'

Meera read the newspaper many times and cried in happiness. 'Congratulations, Gobind. You did it. You look so wonderful, innocent and tough,' she whispered, lovingly placing her hand on the pictures. Continuing the monologue, she said, 'I have missed you so dearly all these years. But how will I face you now? How will I tell you that we're being forcefully separated, that I am incomplete without you?'

She kissed one of his pictures repeatedly and sat up. Tears continued to flow freely down her cheeks, streaking the newspaper below. 'I promised you that I will wait for you. And so, I will, no matter what. No one else will touch me, I assure you.' Folding the papers, she put them safely inside the large wooden almirah. The look on her face was

now of determination, something that could be called the germ of a revolt.

In the living room of the floor below, she could hear the congregation of dozens of women busy singing folk songs accompanied by the traditional percussion beats. As she unbolted and pulled open the door, the sound of drumbeats filled her room. The lyrics of the folk songs became clearer. The ladies singing the old traditional song were blessing the bride to be with happiness and love in her new home. Meera found Pushpa standing in front, holding a tray with a glass of juice. There was a faint smile on her serious looking face, as if she were expecting Meera to give vent to her emotions. She went inside and placed the tray on the bedside table. Lifting the glass and wrapping it with a cloth napkin, she walked back towards Meera. 'Please have some juice. You'll need strength to take on the upheaval erupting within you and your excited relatives outside. Besides, of course, to think as rationally as possible on your next course of action. By the way, all your aunts down below are eagerly waiting to meet you and have requested you to come down.'

'Thank you so much, Pushpa. I am so grateful to you,' said Meera while accepting the glass. 'Please tell them that I will be there in a short while.'

Pushpa was visibly taken aback by Meera's calm voice. Her firm and determined expressions didn't go unnoticed either. She waited till Meera emptied the glass, picked up the tray and stood in front of her again. Looking into her eyes, she tried to read her mind. 'I am seeing a new Meera; someone that I have never seen before. I pray to the mother

Goddess to fulfil all your wishes.' Turning back, she stepped out of the room and closed the door behind her.

After a brief moment, Meera pulled out a bright red dupatta from the same almirah, wrapped it over her head and began to walk down the steps facing the spacious living room. The sound of the folk music increased as she inched closer. But it was nothing in comparison to the loud thud of her own heartbeat.

The spacious and freshly painted haveli was decked up like a bride as well. Lit with hundreds of earthen lamps and decorated with thousands of marigold flowers, the white structure stood like a lone king's palace surrounded by vast fields of rich green crops. Long red carpets had been spread along the alleyways inside the compound decorated with flowerpots on both sides, enhancing the beauty of the ancient structure manifold. While friends and relatives were busy singing folk songs inside the haveli, the local band played popular Hindi songs outside, entertaining the villagers who had begun gathering in large numbers on the plush green, neatly mowed lawns. Tough-looking guards on well-dressed horses and elephants were lined up along the motor way to welcome the guests. A long row of white ambassador cars with red beacons more than adequately displayed Bihari Lal's political clout and financial muscle.

Seeing Meera coming down the long, winding staircase leading to the hall, the ladies stopped the music and rushed towards her. The word 'congratulations' resounded, with each relative trying her best to outdo the other in complimenting the bride to be. Holding her hands, the

women escorted her to the centre stage and made her sit on the cushioned floor that had been especially decorated for the occasion. Moments later, the singing session began with greater enthusiasm. Many took to the floor and began dancing to the drumbeats while others clapped and sang along. Bihari Lal stepped into the hall and stood near the doorway. He looked visibly thrilled to find his daughter sitting amongst the guests and celebrating the occasion. He raised his hands and waved before turning back. Being aware of Meera's affection for Gobind, he was quite apprehensive about her state of mind.

Seeing her father, Meera stood up and briskly walked towards him. Bihari Lal felt Meera's abrupt movement behind him and turned to see her approaching. He stopped. Standing close to him, Meera said in a soft but firm tone. 'Baba, I need to talk to you. It's important.' Bihari Lal was not accustomed to listening to such a demanding tone. He looked confused, hesitated a bit but then relented. 'Of course, my child. But can it wait . . .?' But before Bihari Lal could even finish his sentence, Meera's crisp 'no' came flying in. And this time, it was loud enough to reach the ears of all those who had assembled in the hall. The ladies were now looking at the two in surprise.

The father led his daughter to the guest room on the same floor and sat on the chair facing her. The lines on his forehead reflected tension, anger and shock. 'Tell me, what is it that cannot wait?' Much against his wishes, Bihari Lal somehow managed to keep his voice laden with all the politeness he could muster.

Meera looked straight into the eyes of her father and without wasting time on nuances, she spoke clearly, leaving her panchayat-politico father completely shell-shocked. 'I shall not marry Sujan Singh. This engagement will need to be cancelled.'

At first, Bihari Lal did not believe his own ears. However, seething in anger, moments later, he stood up and looked sideways as if searching for a suitable response. All his efforts to remain calm and polite had by then evaporated into thin air. His entire body shook heavily as he thundered. 'It is impossible! The boy's family has arrived. The engagement ceremony is just an hour away. Most of the VIPs are already seated. I cannot allow you to destroy my image, my reputation, just for the sake of some down-trodden, daily wager's son!' His anger-filled scream hit the four walls and filtered out of the doors to the ears of the women seated not too far away. They stood up in panic and huddled together.

But Meera remained unfazed. There was no trace of fear on her face. With a composed and controlled yet determined tone, she said, 'Baba, I am not a toy to be bartered in return for favours. I am an adult who has a right to choose her own destiny. This political family may add another feather in your cap. However, if this alliance makes your daughter's life a living hell, will that bring you peace and happiness?' She paused briefly before continuing. 'And Gobind is no ordinary person. He's a decorated military officer now. The media out there proudly calls him 'Son of Bihar'. In comparison, what's this Sujan Singh known as,

other than of course son of some goon MLA? If you have any love for me, if you care for me, then please appreciate what your daughter is going through. I will not be happy without Gobind. And I shall not marry anyone else, come what may.' Meera's voice remained calm, soft and polite but it carried an unmistakable underlining of a warning that wasn't missed by her father. Before he could react, she left the room and ran up the same staircase she had come down from, climbing two steps at a time.

An angry father stood looking helplessly at her.

The ladies were mature enough to understand that all wasn't well in the Bihari Lal household. The singing stopped and so did the musical beats. Complete silence prevailed. Everyone stayed motionless and only their eyes followed Meera running back to her room.

Bihari Lal too walked out of the guest room in a huff. He first looked at Meera climbing the stairs and then at all the ladies staring at him. Rubbing his forehead with his right palm, he signalled to his sister Reema standing amongst guests. She came rushing and the two went back into the same room. Bihari Lal spoke to her rapidly without giving any background of the situation. 'Reema, you have spent most of your time with Meera soon after her mother's death. No one knows her better than you do. Please talk to her and ensure that she doesn't take any wrong step. This is no time to send the guests back just because she's in love with some ordinary street boy.'

She responded quickly. 'Please leave it to me, bhai sahib. Also remember that this is not the time to lose your

temper. We need to be extremely careful. Let me talk to her.' Without looking back at her brother, Reema left the room and began walking up the stairs.

The door was shut but not bolted from inside. Reema knocked gently and pushed it open. The two large well-oiled, heavy wooden doors flung open on their hinges without making any sound. She saw Meera sitting on the bed with a surprisingly calm disposition. She was clearly expecting to be approached by someone as her eyes were glued on to the door. Reema went closer, sat by the bed side and extended her hand. Meera accepted it and held her briefly. 'I have just learnt from my brother about your love for Gobind. And I understand that you are opposed to this alliance. But we're in a critical situation right now. I am not even remotely suggesting that you are at fault. But the family's reputation and honour are at stake. Is there any way we can find a viable solution, at least for the time being?'

Meera withdrew her hand. Reema watched her carefully and understood that the little girl she had once known so well had grown big enough to have a clear and firm mind of her own. She waited patiently while Meera settled her stance. 'No,' she said in a stern voice and sat back with her head on her head rest. An uneasy Reema moved closer while digesting the cold rebuttal but managed to keep herself calm while continuing the dialogue. 'Meera, I am not going to oppose your decision of who you decide to marry. On the contrary, I shall do my utmost best to convince my dear brother to let you marry whomever you wish to. But right now, for whosoever's fault, we have a

serious danger lurking over our heads. Sujan Singh's father is an influential political leader in Bihar. He won't take this insult lying down. All that I am requesting you is to think of a way to buy time or else your father may suffer severe consequences.'

Meera remained unmoved at Reema's pleadings and simply said, 'I too have a promise to keep and that I shall. No one else touches me while I am alive. And I am sure no one will want my dead body either, not even my father.'

Being a seasoned lady who had spent wonderful, momentous years with Meera as she grew up in her care post her mother's death, Reema didn't even remotely expect Meera to be bold to such an extent. Her fearless mind had clearly outlined her intent. Deep within, she was happy to see her foster daughter evolve but she also feared for her safety for she knew that her brother wouldn't take the insult quietly. She loved and cared for her and was desperate to find a way out. Moving closer, she stretched her arms and took Meera's hands into hers. 'I have seen this world much more than you have. You've grown up in luxuries that are not even conceivable in Ranjit Singh's house. And I don't want you to make permanent decisions on feelings that might be temporary. In the name of a home, all they have is a shanty hut with mud flooring. It's a bed of thorns, Meera; this love of yours. By the time you wake up, it will be too late.'

Meera saw through to the genuineness and care in her aunt's concerns. Reciprocating with the same gesture, she moved away from the cushioned backrest while maintaining

eye contact with Reema. 'Indeed, I am not as mature, Reema bua, like you are. But I have learnt that '*Kachha ghar kisi ka dekha kar rishta mat todo, ke mitti ki pakkad mazboot hoti hai. Sangemarmar par aksar pair fisal jaate hein.*' (Don't break bonds by looking at someone's mud house for the strength of soil is much stronger. People often slip while walking on the marble floors). If need be, I would prefer to die with my beautiful memories and dreams, but I shall not marry anyone else.'

Reema was visibly impressed by Meera's retort. She hugged her and the two ladies sobbed in each other's embrace. 'I am so glad to see my little girl grow up into an angel. And I am so worried about your safety. Let's pray to God that this testing time passes without leaving behind a disaster.'

Touched by her concern, Meera thanked her profusely and said, 'I want you to do me a favour, bua.'

Reema straightened up, 'Sure, what can I do?'

Meera stood up and walked across the room, opened an antique-looking wooden box and pulled out an object loosely wrapped in white cloth. Carrying it gently in her hands, she handed it over to Reema. 'If something happens to me, please hand this over to Gobind.'

Reema took the parcel and looked inquiringly at Meera. 'What is it?'

Meera smiled and carefully unwrapped the parcel while it was still in Reema's hands. 'It's a small statue of Lord Krishna for my Gobind. May the Lord keep him safe from all the rough weathers.'

'Oh dear!' exclaimed Reema. Her throat choking, in turn making her voice heavier. 'I honestly didn't realize the depth of your love for Gobind. As long as I am alive, come what may, I shall not let anyone touch you. I promise you that.' The two hugged each other again. Reema stood up and wished Meera before leaving. As she stepped out and turned towards the large wooden banister leading to the stairs, she found Bihari Lal standing by the wall. His expressions showed that he had overheard their entire conversation.

The two walked down the stairs without exchanging any words and went straight to the guest room. 'I didn't expect this from you Reema . . .' he began. 'It was nothing short of a stab in my back. I had pinned my hopes on you.'

Reema looked at her sulking brother, heard him patiently and managed to reply with a smile. 'We are making a mistake, dear brother. And if it's not corrected right now, we could lose Meera forever. I have done my best to make her understand the consequences. But it's clear to me that she has a point of view that must be respected.'

Bihari Lal sank into the sofa chair holding his head between his hands. A tense Reema waited with bated breath, not knowing which way the dice would roll. A gentle knock on the door shook them both. Bihari sprang up from the chair as if he had seen a ghost. 'What is it?' he commanded in a shaky tone.

'Sahib, I have just come to inform you that the Honourable Chief Minister will be reaching in half an hour. The local police has just arrived as advance party.'

It took no time for Reema to realize that the servant's voice carried traces of worry and concern, a clear indication that whispering had started amongst the guests. She also knew its adverse effects would be to add fuel to the fire.

'Okay, I am coming. Meanwhile, look after the guests!' he retorted. Then, turning to his sister, he asked concerned, 'Now, what do we do?'

9

December 1989

INS *Mysore*, the training frigate for the navy cadets who pass out from the academy, was anchored alongside the south break water jetty at the naval dockyard in Bombay. It was getting ready to receive the new batch of officer cadets. The training course was set to commence on the first dawn of January 1990. But one cadet arrived well before the scheduled joining date. Climbing the gangway, Gobind stepped on board the warship deck after acknowledging the salute from the two quartermasters manning the entrance. The smartly dressed sailors looked at each other before the senior amongst them stepped forward. 'Welcome onboard, sir. What can I do for you?'

Dressed in simple but well-ironed trousers, shirt and tie, which matched with his blue turban, Gobind politely responded. 'The officer on duty please.'

'Yes, sir,' came an instant response. Picking up the intercom, the sailor dialled a number and in less than 30 seconds, the officer of the day (OOD) was standing in front of Gobind.

'That's some efficiency,' thought Gobind admiringly while saluting the OOD. 'Sir, my name is Cadet Gobind Singh. I have just passed out of NDA and am reporting on board.'

The officer's eyes scanned Gobind from head to toe in amusement. 'Reporting? Now? There are still a few weeks for your course to begin. Why so early cadet; don't you have a home? It's your vacation period. Go home and report a day before 1 January.'

Gobind knew it was coming and was well prepared to address it. 'Sir, I have a situation at home that warrants me to stay away from my village. The NDA commandant wrote to the *Mysore* commanding officer and, thereafter, I was granted permission to join early.'

Alerted by the involvement of big names behind the cadet's early arrival, the OOD became cautious. 'Oh, okay. Welcome on board. But what's that big issue that forced you to take shelter on board a war ship?'

Gobind soon realized that by dropping names, he had unwittingly stepped on the OOD's toes. It also dawned on him that any response of his could cut both ways. It wasn't the best beginning for his training on board the war ship, he felt. 'Sir, I have a problematic situation back home. I have been given to understand that my presence might aggravate it, which, in turn, might cause harm to my parents. I therefore requested to join the ship early.'

Gobind's helplessness brought a thin smile on the OOD's face and also increased his inquisitiveness. 'And what's this problematic situation, if I may ask, cadet?'

Gobind was quick to anticipate and respond. 'That's something I have been directed not to discuss, sir. It is a personal matter.'

The duty officer wasn't amused by Gobind's cryptic response and felt belittled by his flat refusal. The presence of the two sailors standing close by added fuel to the fire. 'Very well, Cadet Singh,' retorted the OOD in an irritated voice. 'These sailors will escort you to your quarters. Settle down soon. My name is Lieutenant Mallan. And I shall be your divisional officer. Interesting times ahead for you.' Dismissing his presence, Lt Mallan vanished into the interiors of the ship, but his threat loomed, giving plenty of reasons to Gobind to worry about. Three men emerged from below deck and ran out to the jetty and effortlessly lifted Gobind's luggage. The top of Gobind's black trunk case read 'Here I come, INS *Mysore*'.

Once inside the large and spacious living quarters, thoughts of Meera overpowered his mind. He lay down on the bunk, tossing and turning as images of their togetherness repeatedly played on his mind. He had little knowledge as to whom she was being married to. He was also sure that the alliance would not have been with Meera's consent. He worried about her safety and wellbeing. Opening the trunk, he carefully pulled out the painting and hung it on the bulkhead behind his bunk. Then, he sat in front of it and admired the painting. 'How will I live without you,

Meera? You promised me and I pinned all my hopes on your promise. Please tell me what I should do now?'

As the sun began sinking into the calm and still waters of the vast Arabian Sea in the distant horizon, the blue sky began turning into a large, bright reddish-orange canvas, offering a spectacular picture. Standing on the deck in track pants and a sports shirt, a tense Gobind suddenly jumped up as if he had found a solution to the jigsaw puzzle. He ran past the lifeboats on the deck and climbed down the metallic stairs quickly. Pulling out a small diary from his pocket, he asked the quartermasters, 'How do I make a call to this school in Patna?'

The sailors were intelligent enough to appreciate Gobind's predicament. The junior amongst the two took the lead and said, 'Sir, please give me the number. I shall connect through the navy telephone exchange.' A minute later, the sailor looked up at Gobind and said, 'Sir, it's ringing, but no one's answering. The school might be closed already.'

As soon as the sailor placed the receiver on the cradle, a navy-blue motorcycle drove in and was parked by the gangway side. The dispatch rider appeared to be in a hurry. Stepping on board, he pulled out an envelope from his bag and handed it over to the quartermaster.' Telegram for Cadet Gobind Singh. Please give it to the OOD only. Ensure the cadet gets it only after he has finished his supper.'

Gobind leapt forward and snatched the sealed cover before the startled delivery man could even react. He climbed up the stairs and briskly walked into the interiors

of the mess. Turning the lever in one swift movement, he shut the heavy steel door from inside, rushed to the nearest table and tore open the envelope. His heart was beating loudly, and his hands were shaking while unfolding the telegram. Instinctively, he knew that it wasn't going to be good news. He went through the text. His pain increased manifold as he went through every word. The paper slipped out of his fingers and fell on the floor. He screamed aloud, 'No, Meera, no! You cannot do this to me!' He sank on to the sofa, resting his head on the table. A few minutes later, the big levers of the metallic door turned again, pulling the door open from the outside.

In came Lt Mallan, followed by few sailors in toe. He looked at Gobind and then at the telegram lying on the floor. Picking it up, he went through its contents that read it. 'Regret to inform you that Meera died in an accident. Ram Dyal Sharma.'

Recovering from the shock a few minutes later, Gobind rolled the painting and packed it into the trunk. He then picked up his handbag and without looking at the lieutenant standing nearby, he exited the cadet's accommodation.

'Where do you think you're going, Gobind? This is a warship, not a company garden that you can walk away at will.'

Gobind glanced once, smiled weakly and slowed down. 'I have not officially reported on board yet, Sir. And as you rightly said, there's still time.' Stepping up his pace, he climbed the gangway and saluted. The two quartermasters gave a confused look and saw him walk away.

Dressed in an immaculate white uniform, Lt Mallan watched him walk away as a mute spectator. He also began to worry about the report that he would need to furnish to his commanding officer regarding this development.

* * *

At the Patna airport, an Air India flight glided towards the tarmac, landing smoothly. It taxied towards the terminal and came to halt just adjacent to the entry gate of the building. Amongst the first ones to exit was Gobind. As he walked into the airport premises, he saw his headmaster waving at him. Gobind ran towards him, bowed and touched his feet. But before Ram Dyal could respond to his gesture, Gobind unleashed a volley of questions. The headmaster didn't reply. Instead, he introduced him to the two sergeants from the military police standing close by. 'They have been sent to escort you to your village, Gobind. There was a message from your ship. Your commanding officer also spoke to me personally. I should warn you that the situation is a bit volatile at Bihari Lal's house. You going there at this point of time could aggravate matters. You're taking a big risk.'

Gobind shook hands with the sergeants like an officer who was in control of the situation. 'There will be no problem, Sir,' he retorted in a voice that was oozing with confidence. 'Please take me there quickly.'

Ram Dyal looked at the two army personnel, and together they began walking towards the waiting military

Jeep. Gobind sat in the headmaster's car while the jeep tailed behind as an escort vehicle. 'No one knows what really transpired . . .' began Ram Dyal. 'It seems that there was an altercation between father and daughter after which Meera locked herself in the room and shot herself with a double barrel gun.' Gobind listened in silence. His heart was broken; his fingers were sinking deeper into the front seat cushions in desperation as he tried to take control of his own emotions.

An hour later, the car turned towards a narrow path. From a distance, one could see the huge structure of the haveli in shades of dark grey and black. There were no lights and the entire narrow lane wore a deserted look. The escort Jeep took the lead and went past the outer security gate without being stopped by the guards. Seeing the olive-green military Jeep approaching the haveli, the sentry had lifted the barricade without inquiring. Both the vehicles sped on the dusty track and stopped at the porch. The sergeants emerged first, smartly slinging their weapons onto their shoulders. The white ambassador car came in next and immediately became the centre of attention for over a hundred mourners sitting on the lawn.

Bihari Lal stood up and walked past the people to meet the visitors. But as he saw Gobind stepping out of the car, he froze in his tracks. He looked at the army personnel and then the headmaster before his eyes came to rest on Gobind's tall and athletic frame. There was a hushed silence all round. Without batting an eye lid, Gobind walked towards Bihari Lal and touched his feet. 'If I am

to be blamed, Baba, then I too should go the same way,' spoke Gobind in a voice filled with emotion and pain. 'I don't want to live without Meera.' He was weeping uncontrollably.

The village head was taken aback by Gobind's raw courage and moving words. His tears melted Bihari Lal's heart even as his loyalist security guards standing amongst the mourners looked on ferociously. He embraced Gobind, letting go of the emotions within. 'I'm her murderer, I killed my daughter, my only child. And I am so sorry. I failed miserably to read her mind, my son,' he said while sobbing heavily.

The two stayed hugging each other for a while, sobbing their sorrows away till Gobind spoke again. 'Baba, can I see Meera?'

Bihari Lal separated from him and wiping his tears with the white cotton muffler on his shoulder looked at Reema, who came running. 'Please take Gobind to Meera.'

Reema gestured and began walking towards the living room. Gobind bowed to Bihari Lal and began following Reema. Slowing down a bit, Reema let him come closer till he was almost alongside and spoke softly. 'Meera loved you dearly. Surprisingly, no one could actually fathom the depth of her love for you. I was shocked to see her resolve to be married only to you and no one else. She has left a packet for you. I shall go and bring it just now.' Reema escorted Gobind to where Meera's body rested in state on the floor. Sandalwood smoke emitting from the trays near Meera's head was engulfing the room, creating a cloud-

like cover. At Reema's gesture, the pundits and visitors sitting around Meera's body hurriedly left the hall, leaving Gobind alone.

He went closer to see Meera's face, calm, composed and content. It looked as if she was happy with her actions. There were no signs of regret. By the shape of the white sheet covering her body, Gobind could make out that she had shot herself in the heart. He sat down on the floor near her and held her hand. Bowing low, he wept bitterly. Reema came back, respectfully holding a parcel in her hands. Sitting next to him, she placed it in his lap and put her left hand on Gobind's turban. 'I am proud of Meera to have chosen the right man for herself. My brother made a mistake and his bloated ego damaged you both. I also found a letter in her room that she wrote for you. I have read it. For Meera's sake, please do what she has so lovingly put it on paper.'

Reema stepped out first, followed by Gobind. The huge crowd gathered on the lawns was now standing, looking at the young and tall turbaned solider coming down the haveli's steps. Even the ferocious-looking guards were no longer looking vicious. He went past the crowd assembled on the lawn to his left and walked towards the cowshed. The caretaker saw him coming and, as if on a cue, unhooked the two bulls. Hira and Moti at first couldn't make much of it and kept standing. But soon as they saw and smelled Gobind, they gently moved towards him. Moments later, they were on either side of Gobind who was talking to them as if they could understand his language. Almost the

entire village looked awe struck seeing their chemistry. He hugged and kissed them on their foreheads and walked them back to the shed. As he returned to come face to face with the Sarpanch, he found that the military police guards were in alert position. Gobind went straight to Bihari Lal, bowed low and said in a soft but clear voice. 'I have a request to make, Baba. Meera can't be wrapped in a white cloth. Our souls were married. However small my house is, she must depart from there, her home, duly clad in a red saree. As her husband, it is my duty to perform the last rights. And that was Meera's last wish too.'

A stunned Bihari Lal looked at Meera's letter in disbelief. Without reading its contents, he spoke in a shock-filled heavy voice. 'What a blunder I have committed, my son! Please forgive me for I am the sole culprit. Yes, Meera will depart from your home as your bride as she always wanted to be.'

As soon as he gave his approval, Reema rushed inside to make the necessary arrangements. A few ladies too followed her. People began talking in hushed voices, many covering their faces with their hands as if something absolutely unspeakable had been said. Bihari Lal looked around and turned towards the gathered crowd. With joined palms, he gestured them to sit down and began addressing them. 'My daughter, Meera, and Gobind, son of Shri Ranjit Singh ji, were attracted to each other, so much so that they had decided to be married once Gobind completed his training and became a military officer. But this wasn't acceptable to the egoist father in me. It was like a blot on my high

status, dignity and pride, I felt. As a result, I have lost my daughter forever. While I deeply regret my decision, I shall fulfil Meera's desire to be known as Gobind's bride. Maybe this way my only child will forgive me for the unforgivable offence that I have committed. My son-in-law, Gobind Singh, will perform all the rituals. I humbly request you to please join us for the last rites.'

Clad in a red saree, with *sindoor* on her forehead, like all Hindu married women would proudly wear, Meera's final journey began from the small cottage of Gobind. Holding one of the legs of the bed on which Meera lay was her very own Gobind, now designated as her husband. In any small village, this would have been an impossible ritual to even conceive, but Gobind's love for Meera had stood the acid test, forcing Bihari Lal to rethink rationally. The procession went up to the temple enroute for offering prayers. Following Meera's request to the tee, the bed was then placed on the cart to be pulled by her favourite Hira–Moti.

'I know you will come, no matter what. Dress me as your bride and ensure that our Hira–Moti take me to the final journey.'

That is what her handwritten note stated.

10

Gobind re-joined the ship before the D-Day of 1 January 1990. He had never sailed in the ocean and, therefore, had always wanted to see how the infinite vastness of the bluish salt water stayed within its boundaries and did not spill over the land, submerging the earth at will. The stark white uniforms studded with golden stripes that the officers wore was an added attraction in addition to the majestic, mighty steel grey warships that rode the waves and protected the shores. Besides, and more importantly, Meera had a great liking for the naval uniform, and that alone was a good enough reason for Gobind to be part of the Indian Navy.

Gobind was commissioned as an officer on 1 January 1991. He had excelled in the training courses and, two years later, was posted to a frontline warship frigate in Bombay (now Mumbai). Standing on the forecastle in the wee hours during routine sailing, he looked at the rising sun on

the horizon. But deep within, his eyes and heart were still searching for Meera. The strong breeze and rising waves were hitting the ship's bow at regular intervals, spraying sea water across the green metallic deck. Holding the guard rails with both hands, he stood his ground and kept gazing at the big orange fire ball that was emerging on the distant horizon and turning brighter with every passing minute.

On the bridge, the commanding officer, Captain Bhanushali, was seated in a plush chair, sipping tea and looking at his youngest officer braving the onslaught of the strong sea spray as if it were flower petals being showered upon him from the heavens. He looked sideways at the officer on watch (OOW), who came running. 'Please ask Gobind to come to my cabin.' The captain stood up and walked down the stairs.

'Aye, aye, Captain,' replied the OOW and dialled the intercom. Moments later, a smartly dressed sailor was seen running to the forecastle with a yellow slip. Without expressing surprise, Gobind walked behind the sailor and entered through the starboard door.

'Good morning, sir. Sub. Lt Gobind Singh reporting, sir.' The CO looked up at the tall, lanky figure standing at the door and gestured with his hand.

'Come in please and take a seat.' Gobind did as told and waited for the next directive. It was a medium-sized wood-panelled cabin, exclusively designed and decorated, befitting the stature of its occupant. Electronic gadgets and communication systems were fitted on the bulkhead in such a manner that the captain could access the bridge

by simply extending his arm. Behind him was a small, collapsible partition and behind that was a king-size bed, which was also fitted with numerous headphones and electronic devices.

'I have been closely observing you for many months now. Your eagerness to learn, your dedication, intelligence and devotion to the service is way above your age. You're soft spoken, well-behaved and possess every quality that any captain would desire and hope for.' The CO paused briefly, letting Gobind digest the rare compliments he was being showered with, and continued, 'But there's something that I have not been able to quite fathom. Given that we are like a large family on board this ship, I would like to know the reason for the pain in your eyes and often keeps you aloof. It appears to me that deep within, you're carrying some hurt, possibly a memory that you're unable to deal with. Can I be of any help, son?'

Gobind was touched by the deep affection his boss was showering upon him. He somehow tried to wear a straight face, to remain composed and made efforts to control his reactions. But his efforts were not enough to hide his changing facial expressions from the trained eyes of the old sea horse. Before he could begin, the steward walked into the cabin holding a fine bone china tea set on a wooden tray. Gobind lifted the cup, poured some milk and added a spoonful of sugar while maintaining a calm posture and kept stirring the tea with the tiny spoon till his CO took the first sip. Thoughtfully, he began with his explanation, 'Sir, there's nothing that can't be addressed. It's just that

I come from the weaker section of society. I am therefore carrying some baggage on my mind that is not easy to shed. Some scars take time to heal. It's just a matter of time. I am sure that I will succeed. I am grateful for your concern, sir.'

The captain heard him intently and the expressions on his face clearly showed that he wasn't convinced with his subordinate's response. He smiled faintly and continue, 'Son, this baggage of yours isn't small. That I can tell blind-folded. But I wish you strength to overcome whatever it is. I am sure you'll emerge stronger from this upheaval. Feel free to let me know if I can be of any assistance.' The captain was in the process of placing his teacup on the side table, a subtle hint that the meeting was coming to an end, when he heard Gobind's voice again. He looked up.

'Sir, I have a request to make.'

The CO nodded and smiled gently. 'Please tell me.'

'I request permission to volunteer for the submarine arm.'

The captain looked surprised. Placing the cup firmly on the mat lest it slip due to the ship's constant see-saw movement, he paused for a brief moment and with a questioning look asked, 'Why subs?'

'Sir, I am aware that it's a tough, demanding and challenging life out there, especially when I feel so blessed to be under your supervision. But I think it's time for me to see my own shadow. And for that, I must stand in the open sun.'

Captain Bhanushali looked into the eyes of the young officer seated in front with admiration and felt touched by

his resolve to fight the battle on his own terms. Standing up, he extended his hand, shook Gobind's and patted him on the shoulder. 'I am sure that you will be an asset to our submarine arm. Go right ahead. I shall send my recommendations. All the best.'

Gobind saluted smartly, turned back and headed straight for his cabin. Opening a small handbag, he pulled out Meera's painting and looked at the vast, blue, choppy sea through the port hole. The waves were intermittently hitting the glass pane, leaving behind scores of drops of salty water to trickle back into the ocean till the next wave came smashing in. Gobind, however, showed no interest in looking at nature's majestic act. His mind had drifted to the one face he had been missing. Turning his head away and resting it on the pillow, he softly murmured, 'I am missing you, Meera, more than ever before. It seems I am waiting for you across the deserts of the blue sea. I wonder if I can ever forget you, even when I am beneath the ocean.'

* * *

Gobind joined the submarine arm, and after fifteen months of gruelling training, in which he was able to prove his mettle yet again, he was promoted to the rank of a lieutenant and earned a selection for an overseas appointment in his very first posting. Impressed by his dedication, the submarine commander of the Western Naval Command handpicked him to be part of the commissioning crew, designated to bring home a state-of-

the-art submarine from Russia. Being a crucial and tactical appointment and given the sensitivity attached to the task, Lt Gobind Singh was asked to appear in person before Rear Admiral Bhaskar Rao.

Acknowledging Gobind's salute and without wasting time on pleasantries, the admiral began in a polite but firm tone. 'I have heard good things about you. You've more than proven yourself in the submarine warfare school. I'm glad to have you with us. You will be the youngest officer to join the team to bring home a brand-new submarine from Russia. You will be trained in Leningrad. Needless to say, I expect the highest degree of secrecy, personal conduct and discipline. There's absolutely no room for excuses or failure. Any questions?'

Gobind sat down soon after the admiral occupied his chair. But even while seated, he maintained an attentive posture, keeping his arms taut while resting them smartly on his knees. Responding in the utmost respectful manner, he said, 'Sir, I am thankful for the confidence and trust imposed in me. I won't be found wanting,' and waited for the admiral to conclude his formal customary pep talk.

But the admiral was in no hurry. He stood up and walked back to his desk, picked up a cigar and carefully unwrapped the silver foil. Like a seasoned smoker, he cut the top end with one click of the cutter, lit it with a shiny, gold-plated lighter, took one long drag and let the thick dark smoke engulf the air-conditioned room. Satisfied, with his act, he slowly returned to the sofa chair to find Gobind waving his right hand gently, waving the cigar

smoke away. 'Oh, I am so sorry,' said the admiral and quickly put it out. Placing it on the ashtray, he continued. 'I am told that you've come from a humble background, worked hard, topped the school exams and then went on to earn the President's gold medal at the NDA. You're an ace swimmer and have been given the blazer on more than one occasion. That's quite impressive, in fact brilliant, to say the least.'

Gobind wasn't prepared for such an in-depth observation and appreciation coming from a top-ranking officer. Instinctively and rather uneasily, he tried to read what the rear admiral was trying to communicate without putting his thoughts in words. Gobind looked at the submarine commander who, by then, had leaned slightly forward to listen to his response.

'Sir, my father is a daily wager. And he's quite proud to earn his two square meals and support the family. My mother isn't educated either. She looks after the home. But, together, they have given me whatever they ever possessed so that I could fulfil my and their dreams. What I have achieved till date is primarily a result of their sacrifices and prayers. They have pinned their hopes on me. And I shall not leave any stone unturned to fulfil them.'

'Good, very good. I am truly touched,' replied the rear admiral with a distinct hesitation in his voice, realizing that he had mistakenly touched a raw nerve. Making amends, he quickly switched to a motivational tone and said, 'Keep this fire burning. Your forthcoming assignment is arguably the most challenging one yet. Not everyone can become a

submariner. Once in Russia, you will be required to oversee everything through a microscope. Ensure that we get the best. Every piece of equipment would need to be tried and tested for battle worthiness. Ensure that even the smallest of the gadgets, electronics and equipment are in a fit and fighting condition. War spares and emergency reserves must be thoroughly accounted for. Read every manual, every book carefully. You have been handpicked like everyone else after a great degree of research. Only your skills will make you valuable from hereon.' The admiral paused and sank further in his sofa to see the effects of his sermons on the lieutenant before continuing.

'Once you're on board, you are in the same boat with everyone, quite literally. You will eat the same food, sleep on the same-sized bunks, wear the same uniform and meet the same colleagues day in, day out. And unlike in ships, there's no escape from a colleague you don't like. Only a win-win attitude will help your cause. In case we run short of any food item then no one gets it. Period. The same law shall apply to all. You will surface and dive together.'

Gobind listened to the admiral attentively. From a simple, formal two-minute conversation that he had expected his formal calling on to be, it had turned into a serious, unending monologue. He nodded gently. 'Aye, aye, sir.' His voice carried the confidence that the submarine commander would have expected to hear.

'Good,' came a quick response. 'You may go now. Wish you all the best.'

He stood up, saluted smartly and was about to step out when he heard the admiral's voice again. He turned around to face him and waited for the submarine commander to finish. 'I am given to understand that you were in love with a girl, but she passed away on the day of your joining INS *Mysore*, and that unfortunate incident has left a deep scar on your mind and heart. I am told that you joined the submarine branch to get away from those sad memories by remaining constantly busy. Is that true?'

Gobind found himself caught unprepared by the provoking question and hesitated before responding. He wondered why the admiral was hell bent on hitting below the belt. Managing to stay calm, he said, 'Sir, life isn't a bed of roses. In fact, given my humble background, it's quite to the contrary. But I am yet to come across a strong person with an easy past. I have so far emerged stronger after facing scores of challenges and hope to do so in future as well.' The words flew out of Gobind's mouth effortlessly, leaving the admiral thoroughly impressed. He stepped forward to shake hands with the young officer and held it for a moment longer than usual. 'I am truly impressed. My job is such that I have to be doubly sure. Please don't mind. Welcome aboard. I am sure you'll do us all proud.'

Gobind saluted again and stepped out into the open lawns. On his left were a row of ships and submarines of the Western fleet, parked along the south break water jetty. The enormity of the job at hand, together with the responsibility and commitment, had temporarily driven Meera from his mind. Engrossed in his thoughts, he

decided to walk back to his unit, frequently responding to the salutes of the sailors passing by.

* * *

Back home in Patna, Ram Dyal read the letter with great excitement. Holding a world map in one hand, he pointed out Leningrad on the big chart, but Amrita showed no interest. She took possession of the map and the letter from the headmaster's hands, rushed inside and stood in front of the picture frame. Placing the papers at the bottom of the picture, she looked up. '*Waheguru*, please grant him strength. It's Meera that he can't get over. He's too emotional to forget her. Please, I beg you. Grant him the strength to overcome her loss.' She looked up at the deity in the frame and bowed as if seeking permission to leave. And then, wiping her moist eyes with the edges of her dupatta, she rushed back to the veranda where the neighbours had assembled.

A smiling Ram Dyal saw her coming out. He moved forward and took back the papers. Giving her the 'I know what you did' look with a smile on his face, he folded and packed them neatly into an envelope and handed the small packet to Ranjit Singh saying, 'Amrita has a direct connection to *Sat Kartar*. Rest assured; no harm can come to your son now. How I wish our school could be blessed with many more Gobinds.'

Ranjit looked at him with a blank expression and kept quiet. The headmaster just smiled before continuing, 'I

have to leave now, dear Ranjit. Bihari Lal is expecting me. He's hesitating to come into your home, as he feels guilty of not having recognized a true diamond in Gobind. Yet, he always wants to be kept informed about your son's well-being. It's always such a pleasure for me to visit your home. It gives me so much peace here. I shall come again next week. Thanks so much.'

Ranjit bid him goodbye as the headmaster stepped out of the door and then returned to Amrita. Both smiled at each other as she accepted the envelope from her husband's hands and held it like a prized possession.

11

Leningrad, 1995

Gobind walked along the black, long, shark-shaped stealthy submarine parked alongside the jetty, examining every part of the external hull minutely, simultaneously jotting down notes in his diary. He was dressed in a black winter uniform adorned with golden stripes. The navy emblem embroidered with a shining *zari* thread on his white turban stood out like a glittering diamond on the crown of a prince.

As he reached the forecastle, Muthu emerged from the submarine hatch and looked around till he saw Gobind at the far end of the jetty. He stepped out of the gangway, walked at a brisk pace to join him, and, together, they walked towards the quarterdeck. 'Such a beautiful city this is!' began Muthu as he took in the vast, picturesque landscape around the naval dockyard. 'Everything is so

spick and span. The air's so fresh, the city's beautiful and the people so very hospitable. I simply love it here man!' he concluded with a sigh.

Gobind didn't react and kept taking notes instead. Walking a few paces together, Muthu nudged him again with his elbow as his hands were in his pockets.

'Yes, it's so pretty it can be compared with the heavens. Especially when I compare it to my hometown near Patna. Yet, I miss the fragrance of the soil, the fields and the aura of my village. In fact, there's this deep satisfaction that despite so much scenic and natural beauty all round, I still miss India.' Watching Gobind becoming emotional, Muthu quickly changed the subject. In his usual jovial mood, he abruptly gestured him to stop. Gobind did as directed and raised his eyebrows questioningly. With a mischievous grin on his face, Muthu quipped, 'Can you tell me what's common between me and this deadly looking tube you're examining so very carefully?'

Gobind was surprised by the query and casually shrugged it off to indicate he didn't know. Muthu stepped closer and pointed at the jet-black submarine. 'Look carefully once again. And make a note in your logbook. This one is Dutch black in colour, many shades darker than me!'

Gobind burst out laughing, making Muthu happy that he had managed to dispel some of the seriousness in friend's demeanour. Continuing further, Muthu inquired, 'I hope you're coming for the gala dinner being hosted by the Russian navy tonight? I am told that besides the yummiest

of gourmet food, we can also expect a grand cultural show, and the Russian beauties are not to be missed!'

An uncertain Gobind brushed aside his friend's suggestion. 'Since it's not mandatory, I would like to skip it and spend some time with myself. I have a lot to catch up on. There's some design fault in the suction pumps and the pneumatic valves are not performing to satisfaction. I have to make a report to the captain before the evaluation committee board meeting starts, and that's in two days. Please excuse me this time.'

This visibly upset Muthu, but he refused to take no for an answer. 'Listen,' he continued, 'Don't give me this shit. You're behaving as if the submarine won't operate without your inspection. Besides, we have enough time. Give your report to me. I will work on it and revert with a completed report in two days flat. Remember, I scored higher grades than you in engineering, including journals on auxiliary pumps and pneumatic valves. But for now, we are going together. I am coming to pick you up sharp at 1800 hours. Be ready. Else, I will sit outside your cabin. Is that clear?' Gobind smiled meekly and nodded as they climbed the gangway and walked towards the deck. One by one, they stood at attention momentarily to acknowledge the salute from the quartermaster before stepping on to the submarine. Opening the hatch with one quick action, they ran down the vertical steps to the lower decks as if it were child's play.

A few hours later, dressed in contrasting attires, they disembarked from the navy service car near the entrance

of the grand ball room. Muthu was wearing a stark white formal suit, a bright pink tie over a white shirt and a matching pink hat, and was walking stylishly as if he were at a Hollywood premier. Gobind, on the other hand, was wearing a simple black suit, a matching black tie over a light blue shirt and a black turban. As they walked in, Muthu looked at his best friend disapprovingly, 'I must say that you have no dressing sense. You look like one of the dozens of waiters present out here. I say, couldn't you buy yourself a decent suit?'

Gobind didn't respond and did not show much interest in the glittering ball room that was buzzing with beautifully dressed, elegant-looking Russian women. He headed for the bar with Muthu in tow and waited for his turn to order a drink. A pretty girl across the bar turned towards him and asked in soft, polite voice, 'What would you like to have sir?'

'Oh, thanks. Can I have a lemonade? No ice please,' replied Gobind in chaste Russian. Taken aback by Gobind's command over the language, Muthu looked at him in disbelief. He looked agape at Gobind, eyebrows skywards. He looked as if he had witnessed the unimaginable.

'Managing to recover moments later, he burst out, 'What man, when did you learn the lingo?'

Gobind smiled, but before he could respond, a melodious feminine voice pierced through their ears. 'Your friend's right. Your Russian accent is very good. Where did you learn it?'

Both Muthu and Gobind turned around to see an amazingly beautiful and petite Russian girl in her early

twenties, looking admiringly at Gobind. The widening smile added to her breath-taking looks. She was dressed in a white gown that tightly hugged her curves sensually around the waist and loosely hung below her knees. Her long, dark hair rolled down her shoulders, stopping just above the waistline. She wore high black heels that had a tinge of gold lining. Except for a missing tiara, she looked very much like a Russian princess.

'A lemonade for me too please,' she requested in polite Russian to the bar girl and turned towards the elderly gentleman standing next to her. The old man extended his hand and smiled. 'Hello. My name is Karamanov, and she's my daughter, Taraa. You speak as if it's your mother tongue. Very impressive indeed! Welcome to Russia. Not many foreigners speak so fluently. Where did you learn?'

But Gobind wasn't paying attention to the old man. Stung by the fairy standing in front of him, he was dumbfounded. She was a little over 5 and a 1/2 feet tall, was slim and carried herself with utmost poise and grace. But what had hit Gobind the most was her startling resemblance to Meera. Like a robot, he accepted her extended hand and kept his eyes glued to her face. It became quite apparent that he was entranced by her mesmerizing beauty. Like an angel in Meera's physical form, she stood in front, wearing an innocent smile on her gorgeous spotless face. Her porcelain complexion and sharp features emerged through the dark, long hair, like a full moon shining brightly through the scattered clouds in the middle of night. He was stung and

bitten, hands down. Her melodious voice further added to his difficulty in searching for suitable words.

Realizing his friend's predicament, Muthu rushed to intervene. Pretending to cough, he nudged him gently. A startled and visibly embarrassed Gobind woke up from his slumber and hurriedly let go off her soft hand. Finding it difficult to look up, he shyly kept his eyes glued on to the floor. Taraa smiled as she withdrew her hand but said nothing.

Standing close by, Karamanov burst out laughing, putting Gobind in a difficult spot.

'Young man, a few decades ago, it happened to me too. Relax. It happens when you're young.' Saying this, he continued with his hearty laughter while turning towards the bar girl. 'A large vodka please,' he ordered and went closer to the high stools at the bar.

His comment, however, made Gobind comfortable, allowing him to recover. He looked up and found Taraa still smiling and staring at him. The expression in her doe-like eyes comforted him further. He smiled back and, somehow, amidst the rising noise levels of the rock band playing at the far end, managed to say, 'Hi, I am Lt Gobind Singh. A pleasure to meet you.'

Taraa extended her hand, shook his and murmured, 'For me too. It's noisy out here. If it's okay with you, let's step out of here to the lawns outside?' A pleasantly surprised Gobind readily agreed and began following her.

Shocked at what had just happened under his nose, Muthu looked at Taraa and then at Gobind in utter disbelief as the two walked away. Scratching his head, he

whispered to himself. 'Bloody rascal, $100 you spent on this new suit, and he walks away with the beauty queen! What luck, man!' he murmured and turned towards the bar. Perching himself upon a vacant high stool, he looked at the scantily dressed, attractive bar girl and smiled. 'Make me a double vodka please, neat.' Holding his glass moments later, he looked at Karamanov, raised his hand and spoke in Tamil, 'Thanks to your beautiful daughter, my friend has at last emerged from his painful memories. Cheers!' The old man didn't understand anything that Muthu said in Tamil but raised his glass in the toast anyhow.

'Cheers,' Karamanov replied and, together, they gulped down the drink in one go.

Stepping out of the large banquet hall, Gobind and Taraa were greeted by officers and ladies entering into the hall in a long queue. Every officer customarily held his hat between the thumb and forefinger and bowed gently, greeting Taraa while walking past the young couple in the alleyway. Gobind had never witnessed such a custom. He was impressed by the Russian tradition and happily responded to each by slightly bowing his head. Taraa took the lead as the two walked past the spacious, lush-green lawns at a slow, casual pace.

Out in the open, Gobind could not avoid admiring the brightly lit, milky-white full moon that hung from the cloudless skies like a large florescent lamp. Taraa kept watching Gobind but except for exchanging smiles, she remained engrossed in her own thoughts. Gobind too

remained silent but could well hear his own heart pounding inside.

'She is Meera's carbon copy. How's that possible?' his heart screamed. The sound of waves hitting the land nearby told him they were headed towards the beach across the road.

As soon as they crossed the dense curtain of thick, tall trees guarding the lush-green lawns, a vast and majestic ocean made a grand appearance and beckoned them. The bright rays of the full moon reflected on the blue ocean, giving a picturesque dimension to the romantic aura. Exclaiming with joy, Taraa spread her arms and spoke out aloud, 'What a beauty. I just love the sea, the sand, the moon, everything! It's so peaceful and surreal.' She took off her high heels and gleefully looked at Gobind. 'It's so much better out here, isn't it? And not so cold either! It was so boring inside with everyone, just holding a whisky glass and engaging in a mindless elbow-bending exercise, drinking away to glory!'

Overwhelmed by the quick developments, Gobind managed to smile in return. Coming closer, Taraa held his right arm while continuing to walk towards the ocean till the waves touched her bare feet. Lifting her gown slightly with her hands, she allowed the water to run over her feet. The touch of the cold, sea water stinging her feet made her so happy that her face glowed. She gently closed her eyes briefly and murmured, 'You know, Lieutenant, someone once said that the soft touch of these gentle waves belies the belief that ships have been sunk by them.'

Gobind let the depth of her words sink in while they strolled along the beach. Besides being bestowed with enormous beauty like Meera, she too had a way with words. The spectacular and mesmerizing effect of the glowing moonlight had come as an added cherry on the pie. As a consequence, a hesitant Gobind let his hand slip into hers and held it tightly. They looked into each other's eyes and smiled. She responded by resting her head on his shoulder. Struggling with his own pent-up emotions, Gobind let the splashing waves run over his shoes, soaking the socks and the lower part of his trousers with sea water. Sharing little nothings, they walked along, stepping on to the wet sand but keeping away from the waves. Taraa held him with her right arm and gently rested her head on his shoulder as they reached the far end of the beach.

There, Taraa stopped and turned towards him and said, 'I think we should be going back. But I must admit that it was the best time I've ever had in my life. You have been such great company. Never have I felt so secure and happy before. And never have I walked like this with a stranger. Thank you so much!' Coming closer, she stood on her toes and gently kissed Gobind on the cheek.

The loud noise of a passing truck brought Gobind back to earth. Taraa slipped her feet into the high heels after wiping them on the grass at the lawns. And by the time they stepped on to the red carpet at the entrance, many guests had already begun exiting through the large door. She continued to hold Gobind by his arm, while he acknowledged the greetings from the departing officers as

ladies exchanged curious glances. Each step he took on the carpet left water droplets that were falling off his drenched socks, but he didn't seem to care.

Karamanov and Muthu were still perched on the same high stools, both engaged in a passionate conversation with the bar girl. On seeing Gobind, Muthu gestured at them and raised the toast. 'To the best and most beautiful couple I have ever seen,' he announced out loud and emptied his glass in one quick gulp.

Gobind looked at Karamanov who was busy filling his glass. 'Thanks Muthu but no more drinks. Get up. It's time to go.'

A smiling Taraa looked admiringly at the handsome-looking, tall young man holding his almost drunk friend with care. Taking a step forward, she said, 'They have just announced the last dance. May I please have the pleasure?'

That Gobind was caught on the wrong foot was visible on his face. While he was still contemplating what to say, Taraa held his left hand and gently nudged him to the floor where a sea of beautiful ladies in most fashionably styled gowns were dancing in the company of their spouses and partners.

'Go, man, go, or let me take her to the floor!' Muthu was screaming from the bar stool. Karamanov was busy talking to someone, and he didn't even bother to look. Finding himself alone, Muthu gulped down another drink and raised the toast looking in the direction of the young couple. Holding her by the waist, Gobind began slowly. The dance floor was half full as many guests had departed,

but those dancing looked at them with interest. Many were jealous and that was visible in their eyes. But Taraa enjoyed her jig and let Gobind take charge of her as she danced and swung on her toes. Often, she rested her head on his shoulder in a manner that left no doubts in the minds of the spectators that they were more than just friends. By the time the band stopped, they had covered almost half the floor, moving rhythmically.

Reaching back to the bar stool, a smiling Gobind looked at Muthu but didn't object to his gulping down more vodka. He looked at Taraa and murmured softly, 'I think we should be going now, or else, it will be difficult for me to carry my half-drunk colleague.' Taraa smiled and nodded and watched him guide Muthu away to the waiting car.

She walked along till the exit to bid goodbye and kept waving till the vehicle went out of sight, unaware of being carefully watched by a smartly dressed young Russian man. The expressions on his dry face weren't that of a happy person. He threw his whisky glass into the dustbin, and clenching his fists in anger, he entered the ballroom and disappeared into the brightness.

12

By the time Muthu woke up, it was 8 a.m. Despite it being an off day, military life had groomed him to be up early. He jumped up from the bed as if there was an emergency to be dealt with. Holding one end of his lungi, which was tightly wrapped around his waist, he rushed to wash his face, opened the cold water tap by mistake and before he realized, he had splashed his eyes and face with ice-cold water. 'Aiyyo!' he screamed out loud. His head spun rapidly as he shivered, and he hurriedly wiped his face with a hand towel. Sulking for sleeping over time, he burst out aloud, admonishing himself. 'This bloody drinking business will put you out of action one day, Mr Muthu. And then, even your own appa won't come to save you. It's time you stopped boozing.' Wiping his face with the hand towel again, after a warm water splash, he slipped into a pair of shorts, a T-shirt and sports shoes. Then, before opening the door, he took one quick glance

in the mirror, ran his fingers through his hair and left the room.

Running across the lobby, he reached Gobind's room, knocked twice and waited. When there was no response, he pulled out the duplicate key from the chain around his neck and pushed open the door. Being close friends, both had each other's room keys, a practice that is common among navy officers. The room was scattered with clothes and shoes but there was no sign of Gobind. Closing the door behind him, he walked down the stairs and stood at the hotel reception facing the beautiful lady attendant. Without exchanging courtesies, he rapidly fired a volley of questions at her in fluent English. 'Any idea where Lt Gobind Singh is, what time he left and if he left a message for me?'

The receptionist looked at Muthu blankly, making Muthu realize that he needed to converse in Russian. Managing to put the words together somehow, he repeated the question.

'Sir, he left about an hour ago. I think he has gone for a jog. He was wearing a blue tracksuit . . .' Muthu understood what he needed to do. He turned round and left the hotel before she could complete her sentence. A short while later he rushed back into the lobby to find the receptionist giggling away.

Shivering in the chill outside and embarrassed about having made a spectacle of himself in the eyes of the receptionist, he sheepishly grinned. His arms were crossed around his chest, his hands tucked under his underarms

and his legs tightly wrapped over each other. 'It's so bloody cold! *Batti band ho gayi meri* (I have lost my mind),' he murmured as he stood next to the heaters. Unable to control her laughter, the receptionist covered her face with both her hands. But this time, Muthu wasn't in a position to get into an argument. He waited for the elevator to arrive and jumped inside even as the guests were exiting, rubbing his palms vigorously.

Fifteen minutes later, he stepped out of the same elevator door again. But this time, he was fully covered from head to toe in woollens. A thick balaclava covered his face that just about exposed his nose and lips. He went up to the desk to find the receptionist putting her best efforts in controlling her laughter. Avoiding direct eye contact with her, he said, 'In case Gobind comes, please tell him to wait for me. I will be back soon. I am . . .' and then he stopped abruptly, realizing that he would need to repeat all that he had said in Russian. 'Forget it,' he exclaimed in frustration and headed towards the exit. He'd barely taken a few steps when he heard the receptionist call. He turned around to find her approaching him. Walking towards him, she pointed towards the sofa and gestured towards a lady. 'Sir, she has come to meet your friend Gobind. Maybe you can help?'

Muthu didn't need to pay attention to her fluent Russian this time in order to understand what she wished to communicate. His eyes were almost popping out of their sockets looking at the lady sitting on the edge of the sofa at the far end of the hotel lounge. Dressed in a black overcoat,

with a matching hat, gloves and long boots, Taraa looked stunningly beautiful. Lifting the monkey cap, he bared his face while stepping closer to her. Taraa stood up smiling, extended her hand and spoke in fluent English, 'Nice to meet you again. I hope you have fully recovered. It was great to see you enjoying at the party last night.'

Muthu saw his own messy hair reflected in her dark shades, which covered her beautiful eyes. Running his fingers through his hair, he tried to straighten the ruffled hair and politely gestured her to sit. 'Ah, yes. It was good. I had a drink too many. Pleasure to meet you again. How's your father?' Muthu had begun sounding like his usual self, happy and chirpy. Taraa sat down on the sofa and responded softly, 'He's fine. Sends you his best wishes. Says he had a great time in your company.' She paused, looked up at Muthu and began, 'I have come to meet Gobind. Is he around?'

Muthu glanced at the receptionist who quickly stepped back and returned to her desk. Moving closer, he occupied the chair close to her and whispered as if he were delivering a secret message. 'That crazy man has gone for his morning training, while I was merrily selling thoroughbred Arabian colts in my dreams. But I know where he has gone. I think he should be back soon.' He waited briefly and then switched to a serious tone. 'I want to thank you from the bottom of my heart. Please accept my heartfelt gratitude.' Taraa looked perplexed. 'Why, what have I done?'

Muthu maintained the same expression. He paused and took time to pull off his woollen gloves before continuing.

'I have been with Gobind from the very beginning. Like a shadow, I have been with him ever since we got down from the train to join the academy. He has a humble background, and I have seen him dealing with whatever has come his way with dignity and pride. Beneath that calm, pleasant and determined face, there are multiple painful layers of baggage from the past. But last night, I witnessed that one change I have been hoping to see for a long, long time. I found him in such a jovial mood. He was happy. His eyes were reflecting emotions of joy, and his body language was reflecting that "out of a cage" freedom. And you were solely responsible for that one change. I am, therefore, very grateful to you.'

Taraa felt deeply touched listening to what Muthu was saying. Removing her gloves, she took off the hat and shades and placed them neatly on the table in front of her. 'Honestly speaking,' she began, 'I was quite impressed by the gentleman in him. There was this aura of warmth that urged me to step out with him into the lawns. It was the effect of his overwhelming presence that encouraged me to walk on the beach in the middle of the night. I wasn't scared. It felt so nice, unique and comforting. When I woke up this morning, I had a strong urge to see him again, as if I was missing something precious in my life. I didn't know how to get in touch with him; therefore, I took a chance by coming here.'

She looked at Muthu and then glanced at the entrance over his shoulders and immediately stood up. The happiness on her face was a confirmation to Muthu that she had

spotted Gobind. He turned around to see the turban-clad, lanky submariner walking into the lobby. He looked at Taraa, greeted her with a wave and headed towards her. 'Hi, am I glad to see you again! What a pleasant surprise! When did you come?' His voice was filled with an excitement, joy and energy that Muthu had seldom witnessed before. Taraa's response was equally warm. She smiled back, stood up and manoeuvred through the small gap between the sofas to reach him. Instead of shaking hands, she wrapped her arms around Gobind and hugged him as if they had known each other for ages. A visibly shaken Gobind didn't quite expect such an open display of love. Sheepishly, he escorted her to the sofa and sat next to her, fully aware that apart from Muthu, the receptionist at the desk and many other curious eyes were on them.

Muthu realized his friend's predicament and decided to break the impasse. Occupying the chair in front of them, he, with his usual jovial expressions, said, 'May I suggest that you, dear Lt Gobind Singh go to your room, freshen up, change and come down as slowly as you can? Till then, I will give this beautiful lady company. Your room anyway is littered with clothes. It is too big a mess for Taraa to sit there even for a minute. Now will you please rush? We will wait for you in the coffee shop.' Gobind nodded, thanked Muthu and patted Taraa's hand before rushing to the door in the lobby, fully aware that he would reach faster if he climbed the two floors than waiting for the lift to arrive.

'Taraa, I have one genuine question to ask, a very genuine query. May I?' Muthu began in a comical manner,

putting extra stress on the word 'very'. She nodded her head, enjoying the mischief he was trying to create. 'If I am not mistaken, you have never been to India?' he asked. She shook her head. 'And Gobind has just come to Russia for the first time.' Taraa nodded. 'And I also happen to be a witness to your very first meeting last night.' Smiling, Taraa acknowledged again. 'But why does it seem to me that you both have known each other for decades? At least you both are behaving as such. If you can, then please share the secret with this *thambi* also.'

'What's *thaambee*?' asked Taraa in a typical Russian accent.

'Oh, that's my pet name. In fact, most Indians from the south are called "thambi", not "thaambee". But you see, being a fair person and possessing such an impressive and attractive complexion, I want to know the secret for that. Maybe I too will find my long-lost girlfriend in the heavenly city of Leningrad. Now, if you may please share the secret!'

Taraa burst out laughing as Muthu ran his right hand over his face. She understood that he was making fun of his dark complexion. 'You're handsome, Muthu, just the way you are. Jovial, friendly, amazing to talk to and fun to be with. I am sure there's someone waiting for you out there.' Then, she paused for a bit, fiddling with the hat nervously before continuing, 'Yes, I met Gobind for the first time yesterday. I read somewhere that "life is not measured by the number of breaths we take, but by the moments that take our breath away". Holding Gobind's

hand under the bright full moon on the beach last night was that unforgettable moment for me. Our meeting was quite unique because I felt so comfortable and secure that I didn't need to look over my shoulders. And yet, I didn't know him at all. Such moments happen with great luck. And when they do, your heart tells you so. What transpired last night will remain etched in my memory forever.'

Muthu was speechless and completely bowled over by the words that felt like a steady stream from a waterfall. He stood up, bowed and held out his arm. Holding Taraa's hand, he helped her get up from the chair and also picked up her belongings from the table. 'May I have the honour of offering you a nice, hot cup of coffee, accompanied with breakfast if you like?'

Taraa smiled back, picked up her handbag and walked towards the receptionist who bowed gently and assisted her in removing the overcoat. 'Thank you,' said Taraa in Russian and went into the restaurant at the other end of the lobby.

The breakfast was barely laid on their table when Gobind arrived and took a seat next to Taraa. 'Oh, I am so hungry,' he said while placing the white cloth napkin on his lap. A visibly upset Muthu put both his elbows on the table and placed his chin over his cupped hands. 'I am sure you haven't even taken your weekly bath. Couldn't you let me have the pleasure of her company for even thirty minutes?'

Before Gobind could think of a suitable reply, Taraa jumped in. 'Why don't we all have dinner tonight? It will be so much fun!'

Scratching his head with one hand, Muthu looked at her. 'No, no. I don't want to ruin your evening. But please do yourself a favour Taraa. Don't take him anywhere close to a museum. That's perhaps his first love.'

'Done!' came Taraa's instant response, and they burst out laughing.

A short while later, Muthu stood outside the hotel entrance, well covered with the woollens and the balaclava, bidding them goodbye as Taraa drove away with Gobind in her car. He was happy for his friend and looked up at the bright blue skies while praying under his breath. 'Thank you for injecting new life in him, O lord. Please look after him. Keep him safe and happy.' He turned to find the receptionist at the desk intently observing his every move. Opening the door, he stepped in and walked straight to her and offered his hand. She accepted the handshake as a polite gesture but looked surprised. Leaning in, he read her name and said, 'Ms Anna, would you like to have dinner with me tonight?' His Russian was as good as it could ever be. She looked surprised at first and then smiled. 'Sure, why not?'

Not far away, two men in black suits were watching Muthu closely. As he moved towards the elevator, they came closer and flashed their identity cards to the receptionist. Anna took a close look at their IDs and spoke in Russian. 'What can I do for you, sir?'

'Ms Anna,' began one of the two officers who was shorter, but from his body language one could make out that he was the senior of the two. 'We want you to get

closer to this Indian Navy officer, Lt Muthu. Take him out on a date, show him the city and entertain him. He enjoys his drink, so take him to all the bars in town. Your boss is being informed of your assignment.' A hesitant Anna looked up and then glanced towards the elevator that Muthu had boarded and saw the general manager walking towards her. There was an urgency in his pace. He stood at a short distance, wished the KGB agents and waited for instructions. His forehead wore signs of worry. The agents escorted him to the adjoining room where they remained for over fifteen minutes. Meanwhile, another receptionist arrived and relieved Anna but not before ushering her to a room.

'Your assignment is clear. Have fun, enjoy yourself and get Lt Muthu emotionally attached to you. All expenses will be borne by your hotel. Is that clear?'

Anna looked at her boss and then meekly smiled. 'Yes, sir,' she replied and stood up.

'Ah, yes, make sure Muthu doesn't even get a hint of all this. Is that clear?' His tone was crisp and sharp. Anna nodded gently and exited the room.

13

Over the next few months, their love blossomed. Taraa took Gobind across Moscow. Hand-in-hand, they covered the length and breadth of the city and looked like an inseparable, made-for-each-other couple. Those were the days when it was commonly known that the Russian secret agency, the KGB, routinely followed every foreigner. Taraa's two best friends, Tanya and Veronica, facilitated the lovers' time together by keeping them well-guarded from the prying eyes of the KGB. Tanya would dress like Gobind and ride her bike with Veronica, leaving the field clear for Taraa. Gobind began visiting her home and found instant acceptance from her family members and friends. Taraa also introduced Gobind to the Soviet Union's rich history and its journey through troubled times and wars. As Muthu had predicted, Gobind showed deep interest in visiting museums and spent hours on end going through every text he could lay

his hands on. As a result, his command over the Russian language and knowledge of its rich history became near professional and fluent.

While driving through Leningrad's streets on a Saturday evening, Taraa took him to a Hindu temple. As she parked her car short of the building, she saw a few Russian girls and their male companion, a guitarist, sitting by the roadside, playing an Indian tune. The girls were singing a famous Hindi folk song that had a pacy rhythm; the wordings were near electric. As a result, the musicians had succeeded in surrounding themselves with a decent-sized audience. Egged on by the crowd, the Russian girls picked up pace while singing the Sindhi–Sufi song 'o lal meri patt rakhio balaa jhoole laalan . . .' Even though the audience couldn't understand the lyrics, they joined in and began applauding. Many broke into a dance and began celebrating the bright, sunny afternoon.

Holding Gobind's hand, Taraa went closer to watch the singers singing. A few minutes later, she escorted Gobind inside the temple. Surprised to see foreigners singing a Hindi song outside the temple and chanting Sanskrit *shlokas* in front of the deity inside, Gobind sat down in one corner and began comparing the two rituals. A visibly happy Taraa sat next to him. The rhythms were quite different to each other. While the guitar strings were striking a chord with passers-by, the percussion beats accompanying the bhajans was engaging the devotees to meditate and pray to Lord Krishna. A mesmerized and deeply engrossed Gobind stood up and walked towards

the large picture frames adorning the temple walls. Taraa followed and kept watching him closely.

He stood in front of one of the large photo frames and gestured towards Taraa. 'My mother has strong faith in *Ik Onkar*. She firmly believes that there's one God and He is but the only truth. In fact, my father is of the firm opinion that she actually converses with *Sat Kartar*, the true Lord. I have seen many pictures similar to this one in the temples back home. But to see this one in Leningrad, and also listen to a famous Indian folk song on the roadside has actually taken me by complete surprise. Thanks for bringing me here. It's so beautiful and serene.'

Taraa heard him in peace and looked at the large picture frame he was so intently looking at. 'Do you know what's written at the bottom of this picture, Gobind?' She waited till he read the text and shook his head. 'It says, mangal bhawan, amangal haari, drabhu su dashrath, ajir bihari.' Gobind was stunned to hear Taraa recite the verse with such ease and perfectness. Shaking his head in disbelief he held her by the shoulders and looked deeply into her eyes. 'How come? I don't understand. You obviously know it by heart and, sadly, I don't. Truly impressive, Taraa.'

Taraa's face lit up on hearing the genuine praise. 'Please sit. I will tell you the meaning too,' said Taraa. They sat under the same picture. Taraa moved closer to Gobind on the carpeted floor till there was no more room left between the two of them. Holding his right hand in her left, she pulled it gently and placed it on her left knee. And then,

pointing her finger at the frame, she began translating the shloka. 'Tulsidas ji is one of the most revered saints. He must have actually seen Lord Rama in his dreams to have said what he did. In this verse, he says, '"the one who brings good and removes evil, he is Dashrath Nandan Shri Ram, may he bless me."'

It took some time for Gobind to fully understand what Taraa had just said. He had heard the verse on numerous occasions but never had the opportunity to understand its deep-rooted meaning and essence. Tightening his grip over her petite hand, he asked, 'And how did you learn all this?' Taraa knew he would ask. 'My parents did not have a child for a good nine years of their marriage. Then, my mother learnt about this temple. Someone told her to come here and pray. She did, and I was born a year later. I was given a Hindu name, Taraa by the Pundit ji who is sitting at the far end right now. My mother firmly believes that this temple has very strong vibrations. In two decades, she has not touched meat or alcohol. And, come hail or storm, she prays here daily, without fail.'

Gobind was spellbound by her story. 'I don't know what to say, Taraa. I have no words. It's a mystery, this life. And I seem to be unfurling some of it now. Russians believe in their motherland. The Russian Orthodox Church has the largest following. Hindus are below 0.1 per cent of the population. And yet this beautiful temple exists and does so beautifully. Plus, so many foreigners are devoted to the Hindu gods. There's so much peace and calmness. Why didn't you tell me all this before?'

Taraa had possibly anticipated this too. Inching closer even when there was little room left between their bodies, she put her head on his shoulder and began in a softer tone. 'I waited and did so painstakingly and patiently. From the very first time I met you, I knew deep within that you were to be my soul mate. And each time we met thereon the feeling grew stronger. My parents approve of my choice; my friends like you immensely. But I wanted to come here and take the final permission of the lord.'

'And what does your lord say?' Gobind barely whispered into her ears.

She moved her head so that it came and rested on his chest. 'I got my answer as soon as we entered the temple. The song, the bhajan, being sung by the devotees welcomes Gobind to their home. To me that was a clear indication of the lord's approval. And the last song they just completed says that I am with my Gobind. My heart too believes it. You're my God-sent soul mate, my Gobind. And that's it.'

'Shouldn't you take some more time, Taraa? You're the most beautiful woman I have ever seen. Being the only child of your loving parents, you have everything going for you. You have wealth, social status, a large bungalow and every luxury that a princess truly deserves. I don't possess any of these. On the contrary, I don't even have a suitable accommodation back home. And you must know that due to similar reasons, I have suffered in the past. Meera was my soul mate. But she too came from a wealthy family. And society snatched her from me. It would be very difficult for me to face this hurt the second time. Please don't be in a

rush. You have ample time. We are great friends and will remain so. And I love you from the bottom of my heart. But that won't be enough. You'll need to be practical.'

But Taraa was no longer listening. Shutting her eyes, she sat motionlessly. Admiring her devotion and overawed by the depth of her spirituality, he decided to let nature take its course. Besides, he was deeply in love with her and could see the shadow of Meera in her. So much so that the very thought of separation made him go weak in his knees. After completing the rituals, the head priest walked across the narrow pathway and stood in front of them. Gobind nudged Taraa, who opened her eyes immediately. The priest smiled and offered *prasad*, which was readily accepted by both.

The head priest sat down cross-legged in front of them, making Taraa adjust her posture. She lifted her head up but continued to rest it on Gobind's shoulder. The head priest was an aged Russian who had served the temple for many decades. He had applied a thin U made of sandalwood paste on his white forehead. It matched the colour of the muslin clothes he was wearing. However, his eyes were most impressive with a humble, yet deeply penetrating gaze that seemed to look deep into the devotees' hearts. Gobind joined his palms and greeted him in the traditional Indian style. Taraa did the same. The head priest placed his tray on the carpet and smiled.

'Namaskar. Welcome to the temple, dear Gobind. What a wonderful name you have. I am so happy to meet you and to see you both together. There are questions on your mind that are bothering you. I thus took the liberty

of coming over to answer them. I have known Kishnav, Taraa's mother for a long time. In fact, I know her entire family personally. Though I firmly believe that a brilliant mind that speaks cannot be compared to a special heart that listens, I wish to share a famous story that shall ease the ongoing trauma in your mind'.

Gobind shifted his stance just to be more attentive. He was also taken aback by the head priest's comments about his being disturbed. 'How did the priest know what's going on within me?' he pondered but kept quiet. The head priest began in a polite, soft tone. 'You are relaxed in an aeroplane though you do not know the pilot. You are relaxed in a ship though you do not know the captain. You are relaxed in a train and a bus without knowing the driver. Likewise, just relax in your life and know that the Lord is its controller.' The priest became silent and looked at both of them. The widening smile on his face became more mysterious and energetic.

Gobind stood up slowly, helping Taraa in the process and then bent low to touch the feet of the priest. 'Sir,' he began, 'your words have just given me a new lease of life. I don't know how you did it, but I don't wish to know it either. My mother has always said that the lord has his ways. The very fact that I am here, in a temple in Russia, being blessed by a noble soul, is in itself a mystery. Your teachings have but giving enormous strength to my wings. I am so grateful to you and to *Sat Kartar*.'

The priest raised his hands and blessed him by placing them on top of his turban. He then lifted the tray and blessed Taraa before heading back to his quarters. They

both saw him walk away and followed behind him till he vanished somewhere inside. A beaming Taraa turned towards Gobind and said in an excited voice. 'How did you like our temple and our head priest? Do you now believe that I was right all along? Or do you still have any questions?' Gobind remained quiet, but his smile told Taraa what she needed to know. Instinctively, they bowed together before the picture and left the temple.

Back on the street, Taraa became cautious and began looking over her shoulders every now and then. 'What happened?' inquired Gobind.

'I think we are being followed. I've had this feeling for quite some time now. But I've become sure now. Don't look behind. Let's call a cab and go home. My father will know how to handle this problem.'

A few minutes later, the two sat in a limousine and headed for her home. From the rear-view mirror, Taraa saw a car tailing them. More importantly, those who were chasing them were making every effort to ensure that Taraa too realized that she was being followed. Their cab made a few sharp turns before arriving in front of huge steel gates. The guard emerged from inside, saw Taraa and pressed the buttons. The gates were flung open and the cab drove in. The tailing car slowed down to a nearby stop briefly before speeding away. A nervous Taraa stepped out and ran inside holding Gobind's hand while the cab driver engaged with the guards to settle the fare.

Karamanov listened to Taraa patiently as her voice echoed inside the high-ceiling living room. Gobind sat

unperturbed as if there was nothing to worry about. He had, however, become tense after seeing Taraa's rich lifestyle and began wondering how she would be able to adjust in his small cottage. Karamanov's commanding voice broke through his thoughts, and he looked at him. 'I have a feeling it's Dimitrinov who's trying to send me a message. He has been chasing me for quite some time now. He wants his son to be married to you. Not a bad proposal, honestly. He's politically well-connected and reasonably well to do. But if my daughter likes someone else, then so be it.'

Taraa clasped Gobind's hand tightly who was still trying to grasp Taraa's wealthy background amidst the glittering display of wealth. He began feeling depressed.

'Did you hear, Gobind? she screamed in excitement. 'Papa has given us thumbs up to get married. Oh, thank you, Papa; thank you so very much!' She gushed, stood up and hugged her father joyfully. Gobind shook hands with Karamanov, but before sitting back, he requested his father-in-law to be to give him a patient hearing.

Taraa disagreed and bluntly said 'no' to her father. But Karamanov overruled his daughter's wishes with an equally firm and emphatic 'yes' and ushered Gobind inside his palatial home.

The three sat across each other on a large round table in the library located adjacent to the massive living room that they were in. He listened to Gobind's past history with intense attention and kept nodding every now and then. An admiring smile broke on his lips when Gobind concluded

by saying, 'It's a beautiful life journey that we all are blessed with. It's the weight of our baggage that slows us down.'

Karamanov stood up from his chair, walked around the table and hugged him. 'I like your honesty and courage, son. I am more than convinced that you're just the right partner for my beautiful daughter. You have a dream and a matching will power to fulfil your mission. Life's principals are simple. Never think you're nothing or everything. Just that you're something who can achieve everything. Once upon a time, I was a poor man too. I simply followed my heart. As regards my foes out there, I shall see to it that Dimitrinov doesn't bother you both again. Taraa, please look after him and tell my chauffeur to drive him to his hotel. See you soon, son. And take good care of my daughter.'

Karamanov climbed up the stairs in a cheerful mood, humming a Russian song in glee. Taraa took a wild leap straight into the Gobind's arms. 'Didn't I tell you that my father will handle it?'

He smiled and embraced her. 'I thank the Lord and hope it stays that way, even as I am a bit concerned. But let's cross the next bridge when we come to it.'

They celebrated the moment over a glass of champagne and ate a sumptuous meal before Taraa saw him off in a limousine. Gobind looked back through the rear window to find the same car following him. But somehow, he wasn't worried. Instead, upon getting down from the car at the hotel, he waved at the people chasing him. The car sped past without slowing down.

14

Captain Sundaram Raju, the CO of the newly commissioned Indian submarine INS *Sindhkosh*, was pacing in his small, cramped but exclusively decorated cabin. Right at the entrance lay a medium-sized, neatly polished wooden desk installed with numerous short- and long-range communication systems. The folding sleeping bunk with limited space wasn't left free either. Similar machines, gears, valves, equipment and listening devices were fitted on the bulk head in a pattern whereby the CO could take most of the emergency measures or speak to anyone on board by just stretching his arm.

The four brightly shining stripes on the arm cuffs of his black coat that was carefully hung behind the door empowered him to shoulder the entire responsibility of the crew, its morale, and the safety of the brand-new submarine. This was a prestigious project; its armaments, war heads and the sophisticated functioning of the

electronic-equipment were to be mandatorily kept away from prying eyes. Hearing a knock on his door, he looked up and saw a smartly dressed Lt Gobind Singh standing at the entrance. 'Please come in,' he said, his voice carrying traces of urgency and irritation.

Gobind took a step forward, saluted smartly, and waited with bated breath. Since the CO was standing, there was no question of Gobind taking a seat. A 4-feet tall foldable wooden rostrum stood on the side of the writing desk upon which lay a thick file marked 'secret' in bold. A small platform on the rostrum's top was made of transparent acrylic that tilted by about 30 degrees towards its user to enable easy access to the text while standing. The CO walked up to the rostrum and pulled out a two-page, neatly typed note. Extending his arm, he gave it to Gobind to read. His wrinkled forehead told Gobind that whatever it contained wasn't pleasant. Gobind rushed through the contents of the letter and handed the note back to the CO.

Taking the documents back, the CO resumed pacing up and down within the confines of the limited space, forcing himself to turn by 180 degrees almost after every three steps. Keeping his eyes focused on the lieutenant, he began in a crisp tone. 'Gobind, you're well aware that *Sindhkosh* is the most important, secret, and prestigious project of the Indian Navy. More importantly, you were handpicked by none other than the submarine commander himself. During the on job training (OJT), you were made well aware of your duties, responsibilities, and conduct. You were also told about the level of secrecy attached to

this important mission. Then, how did you allow yourself to fall into this honey trap?'

Gobind stayed calm and composed. In fact, it was baffling to him as to how calm he was. He responded in attention, 'Sir, I have done nothing that can even remotely compromise the safety and security of the project. On the contrary, Muthu and I have submitted a detailed report on the state of auxiliary pumps and pneumatic valves in the forward block that need to be replaced without which we cannot set sail. I expect a delay in our departure. But before that, the Russians must first accept our observations, whereas they are giving suggestions.'

'And whom did you submit this report to?' asked the CO, alarmed.

'To the executive officer (XO), sir.'

Gobind's response came as a double whammy to the captain. Controlling himself, he stood focused on the first priority and continued while uncomfortably scanning between the lines in the report again. It had been sent by the highest Russian intelligence agency, the KGB.

'Who's Taraa?'

'Sir, she's my fiancée,' replied Gobind, with an impregnable control over his voice that left his captain fuming with shock and dismay.

'Fiancée?' Do you even know what you're saying? Do you have any idea who she is? She is the daughter of one of the richest businessmen in the Soviet Union. Military establishments of both the countries have been marked in this report, which means you were under the observation of

the KGB for a long time. You possibly still are.' The CO went across the desk, lifted the flask, and poured himself a glass of water. Gulping it down quickly, he placed the glass on the table and picked up the note again and without looking up, spoke in a curt and demanding tone.

'When did you get engaged?'

'Sir, last week.'

'Where?' The impatience on the CO's face was now causing the wrinkles on his forehead to deepen.

'Sir, at the Hare Krishna temple.'

'Did you take permission from the command before taking such a drastic and illegal step?'

'Sir, I shall seek permission prior to getting married.'

'Who attended this engagement ceremony of yours?'

'Sir, the Lord Almighty.'

The CO threw the papers in disgust. The two sheets made a ruffling noise and fell in the opposite direction. He sank into the plush cushioned chair and held his head in his hands. 'Please sit down.' Gobind did as directed. The captain poured another glass of water and pushed it down his throat. 'Son,' he began, in a softer tone. 'It's far more serious a matter than you think it to be. The Russian intelligence wants you to forget this young girl, Taraa. Besides, you are putting your future at stake for a foreigner who will not be permitted to marry you. You ought to know that when we join the armed forces, we lose our fundamental rights, such as freedom of speech, freedom of writing, freedom to marry a foreign national etc. If caught contravening any of the rules above, we're liable to be tried

as per the strict laws and regulations governing the Indian Navy. Do you understand?'

Gobind sat still in attention and did not respond. The CO looked at him and waved his hand in the air, demanding a reply from his subordinate. He began slowly with his counter argument. 'Sir, if the Soviet intelligence is asking me to forget her, it means she is not a spy. Since the time I have known her, we have never discussed anything related to my job or the project. We are in love and enjoy each other's trust. I have met her parents and family members. No one has ever discussed my job. They have all accepted me. I can't quite fathom what the KGB's problem is.'

Captain Raju's face fell flat realizing how adamant the young lieutenant sitting in front of him was. But he wasn't willing to give up either. 'Your career has just begun. The consequences can be severe and unpleasant. Do you understand that you can be tried by general court martial and summarily thrown out of the navy? Do you realize that, given your humble background, you may not have a job for the rest of your life? Who will feed you and your rich fiancée?' The CO's voice was now making a perfect cardiovascular graph, with plenty of highs and lows.

Gobind stood his ground. In a polite but firm tone, he replied. 'Sir, it seems everyone is fond of peeping through the keyholes of closed doors. But should we simply open the doors and leave them ajar, no one would even bother to come and exchange greetings. I love her, not because she's wealthy or a celebrity. Surprisingly, this intelligence

agency made sure that we became aware of them following us. There's selfish interest of a business involved. Mr Karamanov told me that he shall sort it out and that we won't be bothered again.'

'Who's this Karamanov?'

'Sir, he's my would-be father-in-law'.

The CO wasn't amused to hear the response. He sank into the chair, holding his head. He had good reasons to worry. Any disciplinary action on Gobind by the Indian Navy had an automatic adverse repercussion on his own career too. 'You may go now,' he ordered.

Gobind stood up and saluted. 'Aye, aye, sir,' and exited the captain's cabin.

The CO saw him leave in frustration. Turning his chair, he picked up the water flask, found it empty, and rang the bell. The steward jumped into action and rushed from the adjoining galley. 'Why is this flask empty?' But before the steward could respond, he picked up the intercom and barked, 'Come in quickly' and put the receiver down. As the steward left the cabin with the empty flask, Commander Adish Behramji, the executive officer, called XO in short, entered the cabin.

'Yes sir?' said the XO, saluting simultaneously as he perched himself on the plush chair. The CO waited for the heavy steel door to shut and lock tightly. 'We have a situation at hand, and we need to be brainstorm. Take a look at this report. Tell me what's your opinion.' He pointed his finger towards the scattered papers and was about to put his elbows on the table when he heard a soft knock on the

door. 'Water, sir'. The steward opened the door gently and entered. Placing it neatly on a coaster, he saluted smartly and rushed out without waiting for further directions. He was smart enough to sense the brewing tension and experienced enough to stay away from the crossfire.

The XO picked up the two sheets from the floor and went through them. His eyes moved over the page, and his expressions changed as he completed each paragraph. Placing the two sheets on the table minutes later, he said thoughtfully, 'Sir, I think we should not rake it up any further. We are ready to set sail in two weeks' time. The fact that it's the Russian agency cautioning us means there's more to it than meets the eye. Meanwhile, we should tackle Gobind through Muthu. They are very close. I am sure there's no harm done yet. Nothing that can't be tackled at our level. He's bright, sharp and amongst the best we have. We can't let a small issue ruin his career.'

Captain Raju pushed his head back all the way till the flexible chair could be stretched and closed his eyes. The XO waited patiently while his CO analysed the whole situation himself. His changing expressions however told the XO that his advice had made sense to his boss.

'I think you're right', began the CO in a heavy voice. 'After all, even the command would ask us for our opinions and not rely upon the Russian intelligence's input. But will you at least ensure that Gobind refrains from causing further damage?' Gobind was also mentioning that he had submitted a report to you about the malfunctioning auxiliary equipment. How serious is that?'

The XO probably saw that coming and was prepared to address it immediately. 'Sir, that's another reason why some people might not be pleased with Gobind. He has refused to sign the all-clear report on account of a faulty genset and some vital auxiliary equipment despite having been put under tremendous pressure by the agencies. The Russians feel that the problems raised by the officer have huge cost implications and can be addressed only during the medium refit (MR) in India. But Gobind is adamant and suggests that we should not set sail without first replacing the genset. Removing the genset would require cutting open the bulk head, which shall definitely delay our departure by at least a month. I have taken up the matter with Commodore Biswal, the officer in charge of the submarine overseeing team (OIC, SOT). He has promised to have it addressed.'

'Let's have an internal meeting on this. Good to see Gobind sticking to his decision. Please see to it that we are in a fighting fit condition before we set sail. At the same time, I don't want to delay our departure. Please call on the SOT and give me the situation report (SITREP),' concluded the captain.

'Aye, aye, sir,' said the XO as he stood up, saluted, and moved away from the chair. 'I shall do that, sir,' he said and exited. As he headed towards his own office, he saw the captain's steward peeping through the galley with a petrified expression. He stopped and gestured with a smile, trying to put the steward at ease.

'How's the weather, sir?' quipped the steward.

'Improving. We're out of the storm, for the time being,' replied the XO and continued walking but not before picking up the water bottle from the steward's tray. Opening it in one quick move, he took a large swig and turned back to find the steward still looking at him.

'I hope it stays calm, this so-called weather of yours,' said the XO.

Minutes later, Muthu was sitting in front of the XO.

The orders were clear. Muthu was to ensure that he accompanied Gobind everywhere and didn't let him meet Taraa again.

* * *

Escorting his friend a few hours later, Muthu looked around suspiciously before boarding the cab. Not too far back, he'd noticed a black car's head lights coming on. 'Bloody hell! They are following us. Didn't know one needed permission to fall in love'. He looked at Gobind and was surprised to find him calm and relaxed. 'What's wrong with you, man? How are you so relaxed?'

'To the temple please,' said Gobind in Russian with a smile and sank into the back cushions.

The cab stopped opposite the temple. The two officers made their way inside through the temple doors. Although trying hard, Muthu couldn't resist glancing back. 'They are surely following us,' he commented as they entered the palatial hall after removing their shoes.

Gobind bowed in front of the deity and sat down on his knees. His face was bereft of excitement or tension. He was at peace with himself and that showed in his body language too. He murmured his prayers briefly, stood up, and walked around the idol leaving a confused Muthu behind.

'Please stay there. Someone will escort you back in a few hours,' said Gobind as he walked away.

Reaching the back of the large sanctum, he saw the head priest holding a medium-sized, brass plate in his hand. He bowed slightly, allowing the priest to put the sandalwood paste on his forehead. 'Namashkar, Guru ji,' he said while momentarily closed his eyes, listening to the priest chanting the mantras.

'May God bless you. Taraa is waiting for you in my quarters adjoining the backyard. I shall engage our other visitors. Don't worry about them.'

A smiling Gobind did as told and without looking over his shoulder, he headed towards the priest's quarter as directed.

Opening the door, Gobind entered into the head priest's small home and looked around. Taraa emerged from the inner room and ran straight into Gobind's arms. They stood in a tight embrace for a long time. Taraa cried and let her tears flow freely, the saline water making an impression on Gobind's jacket. Together, they sat next to each other on the sofa.

Gobind started the conversation with a smile as if absolutely nothing had happened. Taraa reacted sharply

as she squeezed in closer. 'Muthu has told me everything. I too have got it checked. One of our family friends, his name is Dimitrinov, wants his son to be married to me. He's powerful, politically connected, and obviously has his eyes set on Papa's wealth. And, therefore, all this drama. I know my father well; he'll handle it. Please do not worry.'

Gobind maintained a calm, couldn't-care-less expression on his face. 'You know, if ever there's a true love story, then a villain isn't far behind. And that's how true love is tested. No one except the Almighty can separate us. I am sailing back soon. There are a few formalities that I need to go through. Once those permissions are in place, I shall come back. Till then, will you please wait for me?'

Holding his hands in hers, she spoke with a voice that was filled with passion and love. 'I want you to know that I will wait for you till eternity. But thinking of the time I will spend without you is making me feel depressed.'

'Thanks, Taraa. As my mother says so often, it's all up to *Sat Kartar*. And He never lets anyone down. Our pain is real, but so is our hope.'

By now, the darkness had begun to set in. Taraa spoke, 'We have at best an hour to ourselves. My car is parked at the back. No one knows I am here. I changed my car at the shopping mall. And this gown and hat covered me from top to toe. If you like, could we go for a drive?'

Gobind smiled. 'We can, Taraa, but I shall be recognized immediately.'

She smiled back. 'Here, please wear this.' Gobind removed his turban, wore a patka, and covered his face

with a balaclava. He borrowed the priest's gown and, using the rear entrance, jumped into the waiting car. Standing at the front temple gate, the security guards kept looking at their watches repeatedly. They were categorically told to be discreet. Karamanov's influence had begun to show results.

15

Commodore Biswal was pacing up and down in a plush conference room at the Russian Dockyard. Sitting at the long and exclusively decorated table were four officers from the Leningrad Submarine Dockyard, eagerly waiting to listen to the reasons behind the urgent meeting. From their faces, one could make out that they weren't too happy to be summoned at such a short notice. But they were well aware of the status that the commodore enjoyed as well as the relationship he had built so soon with the top Russian hierarchy. They sat on one side of the table like mute spectators and waited for the reason behind the urgency to unravel.

'Gentlemen,' began Biswal in a cryptic tone. '*The Sindhkosh* genset in underperforming and will need to be replaced, even if it means her delay in departure. It's your equipment; it's under warranty, so you'll need to bear all costs. I want to see the new schedule.'

All the Russian officers looked blankly at each other. Sergei Alexandrov was a seasoned campaigner and the chief superintendent representing the dockyard. He was attending the meeting in his capacity as the senior most member of the dockyard team. Without bothering to get up from his chair, or even reciprocating the seriousness with which Biswal had raised the issue, he just looked at the commodore and spoke in a tone that showed his couldn't-care-less attitude.

'I beg to differ with your report, Commodore. I say there's nothing wrong with the genset. Minor faults do occur in equipment and machineries. We agree that in this case they have occurred more frequently. But it still doesn't demand replacement. To replace the genset, we'll need to cut open the submarine deck, the inner hull and thousands of fittings, pipes, valves and circuits. Besides, a new genset would need to be ordered, aligned, tried, calibrated and tested at sea. All this will be an enormous expense, something we can ill afford.'

Biswal walked back a few steps and sat opposite Sergei Alexandrov. 'Then, the submarine won't set sail, Sergei. I can't put her and my men at risk in the open sea. I shall be writing to the authorities about this. Let them decide,' came his cryptic response.

'No sir, you won't do that.'

'And why wouldn't I?'

'Because we have paid you enough so that you overlook minor faults.'

All the Russian officers present were taken by surprise by the superintendent's sarcasm and taunt. They looked

at each other for reactions but kept quiet. Stunned silence prevailed in the large room. A few uncomfortable moments later, Biswal recovered somewhat, slapped his palms on the table, and stood up. 'Well, gentlemen,' he began, 'I'm sad to hear such a harsh, irresponsible and unwarranted statement. It just shows that the superintendent has decided to stoop too low. I shall take this up with the admiral of the yard now.' His voice was shaky and bereft of its usual firmness. He stood up and briskly walked out of the room without looking back. He looked angry but mixed with it were traces of helplessness, worry and guilt. Sitting in his car, he just about managed to utter 'Home', and the black, sleek, gleaming limousine sped away.

Placing his head on the backrest, Biswal's mind ran down memory lane. He thought of when he'd first landed in Russia as the officer in charge of the prestigious SOT. His appointment also carried a clear underlining message to both the navies that Biswal was cleared by the Naval Headquarters (NHQ) for the next rank and would soon be sporting the admiral's stripes. His stature had grown manifold but, sadly, so had his greed of glitter and lust for pretty Russian girls who were ever so eager to please him with any service that he desired. Little did he know then that the favours he was obtaining from the many Miss-World equivalent Russian beauties were actually being carefully funded by the equipment suppliers. As his eyes closed in pain and fear, he recalled his initial meeting with Tanya, a pretty, full bosomed, tall blonde with drop dead gorgeous looks and heart-melting sharp features.

As his wife and children used to stay back at home in India, Biswal lived alone in Russia. When alone, he often went around the downtown plazas in the evenings. He had taken a fancy to an upmarket bar called Midnight. It had the choicest beauties working as service girls. This time, even though his wife was with him, he visited Midnight, promising himself a quick drink. However, as soon as he was seated, he forgot about his promise and got busy admiring the sea of beauties. Tanya arrived from the side door and took the bar stool next to him. By that time, Biswal's drink had been placed on the bar table, which was stacked with glasses and beer dispensers. Tanya leaned forward, lifted the glass in front of Biswal, and raised her bare arm slightly for the customary toast. Her low-cut blouse had much to show and less to hide. Before the bar girl could raise her objection, she took a large swig and looked at her with surprise. 'All okay, girl?' she asked, placing the crystal glass on the bar.

'Err, yes, ma'am, but it's this gentleman's vodka you have consumed by mistake. Your drink is to your right, ma'am.'

'Oh, my, my,' said Tanya, all the while looking at Biswal apologetically.

Before a dumbfounded and awe struck Biswal could react, Tanya ordered a new drink and got down the bar stool. Bending low enough to display her beautiful bosom, she lifted her hand bag gently and pulled out four crisp ₽100 notes and placed them across the counter. 'So sorry for this. Actually, I am in a hurry and just wanted to quench my

thirst. I had ordered a drink while going to the rest room, thought this one to be mine and, without checking, drank yours. Please pardon me. But it's a pleasure to meet you.'

Before Commodore Biswal could even react, she left the bar with a big smile on her face.

He got up, turned around, and watched her leave. The tightly wrapped green skirt around her thin waist revealing the outline of her well-rounded hips, swinging rhythmically. His eyes lustfully followed her till she reached the big doors at the far end. She stopped briefly, pulled on an overcoat and exited without looking back. Slowly, he turned back to find the bar girl watching him carefully.

'Who was she, do you know?' he inquired.

'Sir, I am new here. I don't know. But it was my fault. I am so sorry,' replied the bar girl with a fearful expression.

'Oh no, it's okay. Not your fault. Thank you.' Biswal reoccupied the chair and polished off a few more drinks before getting up. He left a heavy tip on the table, thanked the lady standing in front, exited the bar and went straight to his waiting car. All this while, his mind was occupied by Tanya's sensual walk, her bending down to pick up her bag and her deliberately showing off her assets. As soon as he sat in the car, it drove towards his home. Staying alone in Russia, a country teeming with beautiful girls, was creating a chaos in his mind and generating urges he'd never imagined existed.

At the far end of the bar, two men were quietly observing Biswal's every move. The older of the two softly

spoke in Russian to the other. 'The big fish has taken the bait. Give him a long rope.'

'Yes boss,' came an equally soft response as they walked up to the bar and ordered drinks. Without waiting for instructions, the bar girl uncorked an exclusive bottle of vodka and placed it in front of them along with a fresh set of gold-rimmed cut-glass glasses. Holding the fine crystal tumblers high, they raised the toast. 'To the Commodore,' said the elder one.

'To the Commodore,' repeated the junior with even more enthusiasm, and they gulped down the contents in one go, while the bar girl waited in anticipation to fill their glasses.

* * *

As the car stopped at the porch of his residence with a minor jerk, Biswal woke up from his deep slumber, the overpowering image of Tanya having evaporated from his mind now that he was home. The driver rushed to open the door. He stepped out and went straight into his large, spacious room without caring to even glance at the affluent display of artefacts at every step. His beautiful wife, Shobha, emerged from the side lawns and followed her husband. By the time she entered the room, Biswal had already disposed of his naval cap, his shoes and jacket, and was lying flat on his back. She picked up the jacket from the carpeted floor and hung it around the chair. Going closer, she gently tapped her husband on his right arm and inquired, 'Everything okay?'

'Ah yes, I have a headache. I need to rest a bit.'

'Shall I bring some tea? It will do you good,' she asked patiently.

'No. Just let me sleep for an hour. I have to go back to the office.'

Shobha didn't speak but instinctively knew that there was something very serious that her husband was grappling with. She left the room, shutting the door behind her, and went back towards the lush green lawns at the back, passing through the spacious living room that was filled to the brim with rich and expensive pieces of Russian art and artefacts. Large, fine cut, multicoloured crystal chandeliers hanging from the high ceiling, oil paintings by famous Russian artists mounted on golden, beautifully crafted large wooden frames. Her house was no less than a museum, and their life style was befitting that of a king of a small province. Shobha had often wondered why her husband was given lavish gifts by people he didn't even know, exclusive pieces of art he didn't deserve. But knowing her husband's strong desire for a rich life, she hesitated to question.

Biswal kept lying on the bed motionlessly. His eyes were shut but there were no signs of sleep in them. His mind drifted back to the sensual Tanya. He was mesmerized by her tantalizing walk, deep, appealing looks and her breath-taking sexy figure. She was exactly like a Hollywood diva waiting for a call to act in a James Bond film. He also realized how easily he had allowed himself to fall into the honey trap.

A few days after his first brief, fake encounter with her at the high-end Midnight, Biswal received an invite from the Russian navy for a dance show in the famous Leningrad Presidential theatre over the weekend. Shoba had flown back to India. Being alone, Biswal accepted the invite and went in a smart formal suit as per the dress code and was escorted by a beautiful lady to the VIP enclosure. As he stood near the banister leading to the special suites, he saw a beautiful lady climbing the stairs in the company of another male. By her sensual walk, figure and hip movement, he instinctively knew who the woman was. His heart skipped a beat, his feet picked up pace and his brain refused to see the trap.

As the couple reached the VIP enclosure, they waited to be ushered into the designated box. The brief wait was well planned too and deftly executed by the agents. Tanya looked around as if to take a view of the luxurious lounge below and in the process locked eyes with her target. With wide-eyed surprise, she stepped forward and greeted Biswal. 'So glad to meet you again, sir. And this time, I promise to be careful.' She ended her sentence with a mischievous expression and turned towards the gentleman escorting her.

'Please allow me to introduce you to my husband, Mr Petrov.' They shook hands while Biswal introduced himself. 'Commodore Biswal. I have been recently posted here. Glad to meet you.' And while their hands were still clasped together, Tanya piped in. 'You know, Petrov, I stole his drink at Midnight, and that's how we met the first time a few days ago.'

Before Biswal could react, Petrov gave a hearty laugh and said, 'Yes, I recall you telling me. Hope you'll forgive her, Commodore. She does this to me all the time.' And they all broke into laughter again.

'How come you are alone?' Tanya continued.

'Oh, my wife Shobha had to fly back to India for some work. The shipyard sent me this invite by hand, and I couldn't say no.'

'I'm so glad you did or else we wouldn't have met again. In fact, Petrov is travelling to Europe tomorrow. Who knows when I shall have another opportunity to steal a drink?'

Biswal kept quiet, his face displaying signs of embarrassment. But Petrov laughed yet again as if it was a light comment. They exchanged business cards before being ushered into their respective boxes by the smartly dressed girls in their short, tight-fitting outfits. The curtain was yet to go up, but for Biswal, the showstopper was already sitting in the adjacent box divided by a velvet panel. As much as he tried his best, he couldn't take his eyes off Tanya, who had taken off her overcoat prior to entering the suite. While her husband had stepped into the box, she stood out and removed her overcoat, exposing the bright pink sleeveless blouse that was tightly hugging her big shapely breasts. As she stepped inside, Tanya gently turned sideways and looked at Biswal with a smile that nearly bowled him over.

Like a lame duck, Biswal let himself be ushered into his suite, removed his own overcoat and straight away ordered

a large vodka. 'Cheers,' he said looking at the panelled wall and gulped down the liquor in one go. His blood had been racing through his veins and his heart was beating loud enough to match the orchestra on the stage. By the time the show ended, he was almost sozzled. There was no sign of Tanya. Resting his arm on the shoulder of his beautiful escort, he managed to stand on his feet and walked back to the car. 'Home,' he barely whispered and sank into the cushions of his limousine.

Tanya played on his mind for the next two days, but he didn't have the courage to dial Petrov's number. Besides, it would have been against protocol. He attended office and tried to focus, but his lust-driven desire diverted him to the sexy siren Tanya. He tried many indirect measures to reach her and even frequented the Midnight bar but failed to make contact. On the third day, as he was leaving for the office, his phone rang. The steward rushed to take the call while Biswal stepped out of the living room and remained alert.

'Who? Ms Tanya?' Biswal heard the sailor repeat the name over the phone. Dropping his briefcase at the door, he rushed inside as if he was competing in a 100-metre steeple chase. Before the steward could utter another word, Biswal gained control of the receiver. A visibly shocked steward hurriedly stepped aside.

'Hi,' Biswal said, beaming. 'How are you doing?'

'Is that you, Commodore? Strange. I thought I was just speaking to someone else. But never mind. Pleasure talking to you again. What you were you doing this evening? In

case you have some time, I would like to come over and you could teach me a few sailing techniques over a drink?'

Biswal quite enjoyed her openness. His excitement, anticipating the rendezvous with someone he so madly wished to meet was touching a new height. 'Of course, we can meet and you are most welcome! How about you and Petrov come over at 1930 hrs?'

Even when he was aware that Petrov was travelling to Europe, courtesy demanded that he invite both. There was a brief, nerve-racking silence from Tanya, the effects of which showed on Biswal's forehead. And, then, a faint giggle . . .

'Oh, he's travelling. But I assure you I will be good company. Just you and me. Hope that's okay?'

Biswal's heart dropped in his chest. Breathing heavily, he managed to say, 'Of course, you're most welcome. I shall be pleased to receive you tonight.'

'Oh, so sweet. See you then,' she replied and disconnected the phone.

Biswal sat on the sofa, removed the peak cap, and held his head between his hands. 'Wow, at last,' he murmured. The steward standing close by stood amazed, watching his boss' reactions. Mustering courage, he said, ' I hope all is well, sir?'

Biswal looked and suddenly noticed his presence. 'Ah, all well. We have a special guest tonight. Please get everything in order. Make sure there's good sea food for dinner. Also, get Russian caviar and serve them on crisp toast as starters. I shall send someone from the office to help you. Everyone at home should be smartly turned out.'

'Aye, aye, sir,' came the prompt response and then the steward vanished inside. Biswal kept sitting for a few more minutes, mentally making plans for the evening. He then walked up to the main door, grabbed his brief case, and sat in the car. 'Office,' he said softly, shut his eyes, and began wondering how he would pass the long hours.

Upon reaching office, he called his secretary and cancelled all appointments after 1700 hours. This included a crucial budget-evaluation meeting with the submarine shipyard.

Not too far away, sitting in his office, Chief Superintendent Sergei Alexandrov answered the phone. His face broke into a smile instantly. It was all working according to his game plan. 'Thank you,' he said and replaced the receiver. Removing his designer spectacles, he placed them carefully in the case and gently closed the cover. It shut with a thin click but his eyes were, by now, glinting. The big fish was in the net.

'Well done, Tanya,' he murmured and rang the bell. The secretary came running in, read his hand gesture, and rushed out to the waiting room. Moments later, a dozen officers came in and sat around the large conference table. Sergei joined them and occupied the head chair wearing a proud, triumphant grin on his face.

'Well, gentlemen, we shall stick to increasing the costs by 50 per cent given the prevailing high expenditure on material and advanced technology.' He looked at his men as if he had just returned from the battlefield with

the winner's trophy. Everyone clapped but Sergei's deputy Peter didn't look quite satisfied.

'That's great, sir; it's fantastic news,' Peter began hesitatingly. 'But our contract with the Indian Navy is quite water tight. There's not much scope for us to justify such a massive increase. They will not agree. Besides, we are running behind schedule, and we are nowhere close to achieving even the re-scheduled dates. it's all going against us. How will we manage?'

Sergei's smile broadened. Getting up from the highchair, he set off a chain reaction in which all others hurriedly jumped up as if they had touched a live wire. He waved his right hand in a casual, carefree manner, letting them all know why he was the chief of the submarine yard and not his deputy.

'You've still a long way to go, Peter. These are war games, but played on a chess board. Your best move to trap the King is by diligent use of pawns and not necessarily an all-out attack by the queen. I am sure you'll learn as we progress. The budget-evaluation committee meeting has been called off by Commodore Biswal just now. And our demand for this small increase in funds allocation will stay. I shall see to it. You may go and enjoy yourselves now. Drinks are on the house.

Good day, gentlemen.' They cheered before departing.

The secretary rushed in as soon as she saw the officers exiting through the door in a long queue.

'Take a break, Lily. Have fun. I am going home too. Good day.'

Smilingly, she stood rooted to where she was, letting her boss go first. 'It's all worked out with the Commodore, I presume?'

'Yes, we are almost there. It's just a matter of time. The bait's working well. Please tell Tanya to meet me tomorrow morning.'

'I shall do that, sir. Have a good day.'

16

Tanya stepped out of the cab and into the courtyard and walked inside the large, well-decorated living room to find the commodore eagerly waiting for her. Beneath her long fur coat, she was wearing a tight blue silk gown that showed off her assets rather than hiding them. By the very look of the designer cuts, it was evident that she wasn't wearing a bra. Her slim, spotless legs projected provocatively from the slit of her sleek, tight-fitting gown. Biswal helped her take off the overcoat and handed it over to the steward who tried his best to keep his eyes down and not stare but failed miserably.

'What a wonderful house you have in here, Commodore, and that too at such a prime location! Must say you live like a king,' complimented Tanya as her eyes glanced at the expansive, high-ceiling hall. And so beautifully maintained,' she concluded.

Biswal smiled and nodded but didn't speak, letting Tanya express herself further. 'And look at these paintings!

Rare, I must say. But I feel you need a few coloured and exclusively cut gold-plated crystal chandeliers on the ceiling to complement the dome on the top. It would add so much more beauty to this amazing decor. That's what's missing in your kingdom, my Commodore.'

Biswal smiled. 'I agree with you, but this is a rented space, Tanya, and I am here for a limited period only. What you're suggesting would cost a bomb. Something I can ill afford, I am afraid. But thanks for your honest suggestions. I shall try and address them before your next visit to my humble cottage.'

The steward stood in front to take an order. Instead, Tanya went past him to the bar, took a close look at the shelf loaded with the choicest of brands, and pulled out a bottle of red wine. 'How's this for starters, dear? It grows on you, this robust Italian beauty.'

Biswal's eyes lit up. He went closer to uncork the bottle, but she took the lead and said, 'Please allow me.' With well trained, experienced fingers, she pulled open the cork and poured the ruby-red liquid into the two crystal goblets placed on the bar table. Holding them gently by their stem in her both hands, she offered one to Biswal and moved closer to him. 'To our friendship, Commodore'. Like a robot, Biswal simply followed her directives.

Another steward appeared with a platter of caviar, neatly placed in tiny bowls, square pieces of crispy toasts and thin slices of freshly cut lemons. These were kept between small steel squeezers on either side of the plate and provided a spectacular contrast to the multicoloured bowls

of fish eggs. Tanya's eyes lit up. 'Wow. That's my favourite. Thanks so much. Now that's royalty,' she beamed. 'Cheers,' she exclaimed with joy and raised a toast. They touched the glasses gently and sipped the wine. 'Nice, ah I love it,' Tanya continued as she sat closer to Biswal on the sofa. The long below-waist cut of her silk gown slipped sideways allowing Biswal to take a good look at her naked thighs. She drank slowly, and with every fresh glass, she inched closer to Biswal.

A few rounds later, she whispered in a romantic tone that floored her host completely. 'Let's get to know each other better, Commodore. What attracts you to me? And I know you like me a lot. I have seen it in your eyes. Be honest. I am here because I like you too. And I think you're very muscular, hot, tan-brown and sexy.' Saying this, Tanya gently placed her left hand on his thigh, while holding the wine glass in the other.

At first, Biswal hesitated. He was unprepared to advance at such a rapid pace and was visibly taken aback by her question. But he felt emboldened by her compliments and inviting looks. Taking another measured sip, he put the glass on the side table to his left and said, 'I just love the way you are, a complete woman, sexy enough to arouse a dead man. To me, you're the most beautiful lady on earth. Period.'

'So sweet. Thank you so much! I just love your compliments and how gallant you are! And if you must know, Petrov and I aren't married.' Saying this, she wrapped her right arm around Biswal's neck and gently kissed him

on his cheek. Encouraged by her, Biswal too reciprocated by gently placing his lips on to hers.

At the sound of the steward's footsteps approaching, the two separated in a hurry. 'Sir, when should I lay the food?' This time, the steward's head was bent low; his eyes stayed glued to the fine design of the Persian carpet as if evaluating the number of knots per square inch the fine colourful piece had been knitted into.

Biswal awkwardly looked at the young sailor and then at Tanya. She smiled and then turned towards the steward. 'I think we can eat whenever the food is on the table.' The steward glanced at his boss for confirmation and rushed to the kitchen without waiting for his response.

They ate in silence. Tanya praised the food and complimented the chef after that. Liqueurs were served in the living room, and sipped in a relative silence. The presence of people had clearly unnerved Biswal. He was fully aware of the power of a whisper campaign that could often start from the sailors' galley and reach the Naval Headquarters (NHQ) at an alarming speed. They barely finished the drink when the watchman came knocking in. 'Sir, a car has arrived for Madam.'

Biswal looked at Tanya questioningly. 'Oh, I had asked the driver to come back in two hours. Perhaps he has arrived a bit early.' Then, turning towards the watchman, she said, 'Please tell him to wait.' As the guard vanished out of the same door he had entered from, Tanya put her hand on Biswal's and spoke softly. 'You have too many people out here. Please come to my home. There's much privacy,

and I promise you that I'd match up to the culinary skills as well. How about this weekend at 8 p.m.? It will be fun.'

Biswal was speechless. The sexy siren he had been yearning for so desperately was inviting him to spend a night at her own home. 'Thanks, Tanya, it shall be my pleasure,' he managed to say. The enchantress' vice-like grip on the commodore was quite visible even though there was no one to see.

'Great then. See you soon. Here's my address and contact details.' Bending forward, she quickly planted another kiss, this time on Biswal's lips and, with a mischief-filled smile, whispered, 'More when we meet next.'

Biswal went up to the door to see her off and went straight to his room. He undressed and stood under the shower for a long time. Far too much had happened in such a quick time. There was a feeling of guilt in his mind, but he was willingly tossing caution to the winds. His heart and body were yearning for Tanya. He was smitten by her sex appeal. Her silken gown that was slipping away at the slightest provocation had numbed his mental faculties and stopped him from thinking sensibly. She was a diva who had overpowered him by incapacitating his brain. After standing for a good 20 minutes under the shower, he stepped out, cleaned himself dry, wore a bathrobe and lay down on the bed without bothering to change into night clothes. The officer in him had by then become completely possessed by the Russian Marilyn Monroe. He began planning for the weekend rendezvous with the sexy queen. Before long, he was fast asleep, dreaming

of holding Tanya in his arms, without her tightly fitted silk gown.

* * *

Next day, the large, adequately decorated committee room of the Indian Navy office at Leningrad was filled to capacity. Chairing the meeting, Commodore Biswal addressed the Russian contractors, stressing upon the need for rectifying the defects before the submarine was formally handed over to the Indian Navy.

Seated not so far away, the Chief Contractor Sergei Alexandrov was shaking his head in disagreement. 'Gentlemen,' the commodore stressed, 'the subs are far from ready. If the equipment isn't preforming to perfection, they need to be changed and replaced, even if the bulkhead requires to be cut open. *Sindhkosh* is going to be one of our frontline submarines. We just cannot afford any shortcomings even if we have to delay the commissioning. Any questions?'

Sergei was eagerly waiting for his turn. His tone contained traces of aggression and entitlement. 'Commodore, tell me, who inspected the genset? I want direct interaction with that expert. If I am proven wrong, I shall change the whole goddamn submarine. And, if not, you will have to accept the equipment as it is. Of course, we shall be only too happy to repair when required.

Commodore Biswal looked at *Sindhkosh*'s CO, who, in turn, directed Lt Gobind Singh to respond. Gobind

stood up, bowed gently, and greeted the CO and the commodore.

'Sir,' he began in a soft but firm tone, 'A strong and powerful genset is like the heart of any submarine. Therefore, its health is of paramount importance for the survival of the boat as well as the crew manning it. Repeated failures of the machinery forced us to do an in-house inspection, and we found out that the entire genset was a used piece, brought out of an old submarine decommissioned in St Petersburg. Our team visited the St Petersburg dry dock and pulled out the records. That genset's pattern number and markings match the one on board *Sindhkosh* to the tee. We shall, therefore, not accept this machine under any circumstances. On behalf of the Indian Navy, I have the honour to submit this file for your perusal and records, sir.'

Gobind bowed gently. There was a stunned silence in the room.

After a brief pause, Sergei stood up and turned towards the young lieutenant, 'Why are you misleading the committee? Aren't you aware that the genset was fitted on the Russian sub only for a brief period of eight months and then refitted to match the *Sindhkosh*'s requirements?

'So, you agree that it is a second-hand machinery, Sergei?' the commodore questioned. Caught on the wrong foot, Sergei got up from the chair and walked out of the room without saying another word. The meeting was called off. Gobind waited, while his CO spent nearly an hour with the commodore in his cabin.

When the CO walked out of the commodore's office, he was smiling. Then, he gestured at Gobind, who followed his boss. 'You were spot on, Gobind. Travelling to St Petersburg and bringing back the original document out of the dockyard was an impossible feat. You need commendations for sure for saving the day for us. Well done, son. Keep it up.'

17

The car stopped near Sindhkosh parked alongside the jetty. The CO was the first to cross the gangway. Acknowledging the salutes, he shook hands with the XO and waited for Gobind to embark. 'We'll be going back to dry docks. Be prepared for another round of sea trials. Tonight, let's raise a toast to the young lieutenant for taking the winds out of Sergei's sails. See you at 1900 hours at the club.

The XO and Gobind saluted while the CO climbed down the hatch.

* * *

Not too far away, Biswal opened his eyes to find himself covered with soft white sheets under an exclusive handmade crystal chandelier. A tiny bulb in the heart of the chandelier was lit, operating as a night lamp. He rubbed his eyes, gently scratched his neck and chest and got out of the bed.

There was no sign of Tanya. He wrapped himself with the silk gown and walked out of the palatial bedroom towards the kitchen but hurriedly stopped midway on hearing a man talking to someone in a hushed tone.

Startled, Biswal sneaked towards the direction and peeped through the long curtain dividing the lobby and the living room. What he saw sent a chill down his spine. Standing in the middle of the living room and dressed in a see-through gown was Tanya. Talking to her was none other than Sergei Alexandrov. Biswal retracted his steps, rushed towards the bedroom, and pushed himself beneath the sheets again. Minutes later, Tanya entered the bedroom and removing her chiffon gown slid beside Biswal. The commodore tried his best to stay calm, pretending to be fast asleep, even as his heart was beating like a locomotive engine.

About an hour later, he felt a gentle tap on his cheeks. Opening his eyes, he looked up to find Tanya standing with a cup of tea. 'You were sleeping like a log, Commodore. Didn't feel like waking you up. But I remembered you telling me about some engagement in the office.'

'Ah, yes. What time is it?'

'It's 8 a.m. Spicy grilled jumbo prawns for breakfast are waiting for you. Take a quick shower. I shall wait for you at the table.'

Back at home, after a quick shower, he rushed towards the telephone. Without exchanging greetings, he directed the listener at the other end in rapid fire English, 'Call up Chief Superintendent Sergei Alexandrov. Tell him that I

wish to meet him in my office at noon today. Also, tell him to be on time because I am calling on the admiral at 1400 hours. If he inquires anything further, please tell him you know nothing else. Is that clear?'

After listening intently with satisfaction to his PA's response, Biswal placed the receiver back on the cradle. Then, he sat back against the bed rest with his cup of tea, while his mind was far from being at ease. The more he thought about it, the more it became clear to him that he had become victim to a fine trap laid by the arms suppliers' mafia. It was not yet clear what proof this mafia had against him that encouraged Sergie Alaxandrov to be so confident.

Biswal's threat of calling on the admiral had worked like a fire alarm. Sergei arrived for his meeting with Biswal well before time and tried to extract information from the secretarial staff while anxiously waiting in the lounge. At the designated time, he was ushered into the commodore's office. Even as he tried to be casual, his body language did not support his facial expressions. He took the seat opposite Biswal and impatiently looked at his face, trying to understand and counter his line of attack. The chess game was in full swing, and the commodore's queen was in attack mode against the tiny, indefensible and helpless pawns.

Instead of engaging in arguments, Biswal pushed a note to Sergei across the table. He grabbed it quickly and began reading its contents. As his eyes scanned the paper, line by line, wrinkles began to appear on his forehead, confirming to Biswal that his plan had worked. Placing the note on the

table in a haphazard manner, he looked up and saw a calm and composed Biswal observing him intently.

'What are you trying to prove, Commodore? That we are a gang of blackmailers and profiteers? That we laid a honey trap? Remember, I have evidence of you with Petrov's wife, Tanya, and with many other teenagers, in the past. I have proof of having supplied you with expensive pieces of art, dozens of sets of rare cutlery, crockery, air conditioners, exclusive chandeliers and jewellery. We even sponsored your family vacations in Europe. All these expenses were incurred in lieu of just a small increase in the budgets, which your navy shall allocate upon your approval. Nothing shall go from your pocket. It's a simple give and take, an accepted market norm. What's wrong with it?'

Biswal smiled, waited for a brief moment, and then pushed another paper across the table. 'What's this?' asked a confused and scared Sergei as he pulled the white A4-sized sheet closer to himself. The letter was addressed to the admiral of the yard, listing every item that was given to the commodore as a gift and requesting the Russian anti-corruption bureau to take account and possession of the same. A flabbergasted Sergei was rattled by this to the core. He threw the paper aside and stood up.

'You . . . you can't do this, sir. You'll be court-martialled. Your career will be finished. You'll never make it to the next rank. This is professional hara-kiri. You're committing suicide. Are you mad?' By the time Sergei finished his rant, his voice had become thin and brittle. But the word 'sir'

clearly indicated Sergei's admission that he had met his match.

'Calm down, Sergei. Take a seat. I have already decided to take this action, and I am prepared to be tried by the general and court-martialled by the Indian Navy for my actions that were not befitting the stature of the high office I have been occupying. But I shall not let scoundrels and fly-by-night operators, such as you, to spoil the good relations and trust between our two countries, relations that have been painstakingly built over many decades. I cannot let my alma mater, the beautiful Indian Navy, suffer because I fell from grace. I am a soldier and shall go down like one. And my wife agrees with me about this decision. You may go now.'

'Don't do this. Please don't. I will be ruined. Our system here is far more cruel than yours in India. My entire family will be wiped off. Please, I beg you, Commodore. Think again. I shall work out a solution. No one will suffer. I shall return the negatives. Tanya shall leave Leningrad forever. It shall never happen again to anyone. I promise you. Please . . . please have mercy on me, sir.' Sergei was now almost on his knees. All the pawns on his chess board had perished, his biggest strength, the white queen was gone, and the king was checkmated, all hands down.

Biswal rang the bell twice. Two armed naval guards came marching in and stood in front in attention. Without looking at them, Biswal ordered, 'Please escort the gentleman out and ensure he doesn't ever enter this office again.' Sergei looked at Biswal in utter disbelief. Mentally

bruised and shaken up, he managed to get up from the chair and walked ahead of the armed guards. He kept looking back at the commodore with hope, his eyes pleading for mercy. 'Please sir . . . please,' his voice echoed in the room as he exited.

* * *

'Home,' he said, and the driver pressed on the gas paddle. Biswal had submitted all the documents to his higher command together with a detailed list of all ill-gotten gifts. Tanya and Sergei were immediately taken into custody by the Russian authorities. Biswal was relieved of his duties by the Indian Navy with immediate effect but asked to stay in Moscow till the completion of investigations.

The car entered the compound. He stepped out to find Shobha standing at the porch. The driver rushed to open the door. A tired but relieved-looking Biswal stepped out and looked into the eyes of his better half. She came closer, held his hand, and escorted him inside. The living room no longer possessed any grandeur. The chandeliers were gone, and so were the grand golden frames in which there were works of famous masters. Yet, the place looked beautiful, simple and serene. Shobha helped him sit on the soda and served tea.

'What happened is the past, Biswal. I cannot forgive you for what you have done. No one can. But I want you to know that by taking me into your confidence and accepting my advice, you have done me proud. I want you to know

that I shall stand with you, come what may. We don't need this rich and high-flying lifestyle, never really did. Let's begin a new life. Let's together fade away into history, forever.'

Two tiny drops of tears emerged from Biswal's eyes. He stood up and hugged Shobha. 'I am sorry for what I did. I don't know how I will face the world back home.' Saying this, he walked into his room and lay down on the bed. Shobha followed and sat next to him. 'Please know, Biswal, we all are perfect in our respective imperfections. This too shall pass.'

As best as he tried, Biswal could not stop thinking about Tanya. He found himself down memory lane and saw himself stepping into Tanya's apartment, paying her a return visit. It was a luxurious, spacious, and self-contained pad filled with every comfort one could think of. She herself opened the door and greeted him with an intimate hug. Then, instead of exchanging pleasantries, she held him by his necktie and pulled him gently to her bedroom. Enslaved by lust, Biswal simply followed her like a trained dog on a leash.

Little did Biswal then know that it was all a well-planned strategy to blackmail him into submission. It was meticulously filmed by Sergei's agents using high-definition cameras hidden at vantage positions.

Tossing and turning on his bed in deep, mental agony, he realized the huge price he had to pay for his short-lived greed and lust. But without Shobha's guidance, he would have gone down the quicksand and, more importantly,

made the Indian Navy suffer hugely for his indulgences. However, his bold step had ensured that *Sindhkosh* received new machinery and equipment as soon as possible and that they were tested at sea and commissioned well before setting sail for the Indian shores. And, while becoming a martyr of sorts, he left an example of do's and don'ts for the others to learn from.

18

The brand-new and freshly painted submarine was all set for the ceremonial send off by the Russian naval dockyard. VIPs from both countries and Indian diplomatic staff stood on the long, beautifully decked-up jetty. They were all smartly dressed in their respective military uniforms, studded with medallions, ceremonial swords and all the glitter attached to their ranks and designations. Amongst the prominent and visible Russian delegates was Dimitrinov. He came calling by, overruling protocol just to showcase the backing he enjoyed from his political masters. With sarcasm on his face, he went past the captain without exchanging greetings and stopped right in front of Lt Gobind Singh. '*Dasvidania*,' he said in an acid-laced tone and then rubbed it in further by adding in English, 'Hope we don't ever meet again.'

Gobind felt angry on seeing his CO receiving the snub from a non-official visitor. Wearing a thin sarcastic smile,

he spoke in fluent Hindi, '*Apne ehenkaar ko modh kar kagaz ka hawai jahaz banaa lo. Tum sachh me udhne lagoge* [Fold your ego and make a paper plane out of it. Rest assured; you will fly].' Dimitrinov didn't understand a thing, but one look at the captain's shocked face, and he knew that it wasn't the politest of comments.

'What did you say?' he demanded, in an angry voice while gesturing for a translation from the officers standing in front. Finding no response from anyone, he repeated his demand in a stiffer tone, 'I want to know what this officer said!'

Captain Raju intervened immediately. Stepping in between, he directed Gobind to board the submarine, and without responding to Dimitrinov's question, he turned towards the XO, lifted his right hand, and rotated his forefinger clockwise in the air. The XO reacted in anticipation and shouted on the handheld mike: 'Single up.' Like a well-oiled machine, the crew began removing the thick nylon ropes that tied the submarine to the bollards on the jetty. Standing all by himself, Dimitrinov had no choice but to sulk. He stepped back to let the ropes pass through, but his face reflected anger and his demeanour was what could be termed undiplomatic at best.

One by one, the small crew attending to the ceremonies on the jetty quickly embarked on the *Sindhkosh*, the captain being the last one to step on the gangway. The quartermasters had barely finished blowing the ceremonial side pipe and receiving the commanding officer on board when a red-beacon flashing escort Jeep came charging in on

the jetty. It drove ahead of the gangway and quickly came to a grinding halt. Four armed Russian security guards ran towards the approaching black VVIP limousine. The sedan halted right in front of the gangway and waited for a brief moment for the guards to take positions. Captain Raju identified the Russian defence minister sitting inside and rushed back to the jetty before the two sailors could blow the ceremonial pipes again. The officer on duty shuffled uncomfortably realizing the faux pas of not having played the pipes on cue and looked at the XO helplessly. But the calm and composed XO just smiled it off and put him at ease with a gesture of his hand.

'What an honour, sir, to receive you on board. I am highly obliged that you took the trouble to come all the way to see us off. Thank you so very much,' said the captain in fluent Russian. But before the minister could respond, the Russian guards at the other end came marching in with their knee-high leather boots stomping on the cemented jetty, making a unique sound with each step. Upon reaching closer to the car door, one of the guards pulled open the door in a well-rehearsed drill and stood on the side in attention. Unprecedented and not a part of standard protocol, the minister's unscheduled visit surprised the officials and visitors standing on the jetty. They careened their necks out to understand the mystery.

Right in the front row stood Dimitrinov, eager to show off his position and importance. He inched ahead in order to be slightly away from rest of the crowd. But what he saw forced him to retract his steps in a hurry. The wearer of

the immaculately polished pair of black shoes who emerged from the car was none other than Karamanov. The two looked at each other. Dimitrinov smiled and hesitatingly came forward. Their eyes met as he sheepishly extended his arm for a hand shake. In a strong display of tough body language, Karamanov turned his back towards his old friend but not before making a brief comment. 'I have seen happy beggars. I am now looking at a sad millionaire. What a pity!' A visibly shaken and deeply embarrassed Dimitrinov gulped. Retracting his extended right hand, he sheepishly stepped back till he merged into the last row of the audience gathered to see off *Sindhkosh*.

The minister went closer to the vehicle's door and gestured to the lady sitting inside the car. Dressed in a pretty mauve-coloured gown with a matching ribboned Colombian leather hat and black knee-high boots, Taraa stepped out of the rear seat, assisted by none other than the minister himself. She stood next to her father, who walked around the car to get his daughter.

Following protocol, Captain Sundaram Raju saluted the lady and gently bowed. 'Pleasure to meet you, Ma'am. Thank you for gracing the occasion.' The stunning-looking lady politely extended her right hand that was covered till her elbow with a thin, off-white leather glove. The CO held her hand gently but failed to control his expressions that were clearly seeking answers as to why so many protocols were being broken by the visiting dignitary.

'Hello, Captain. I am Taraa. With your permission, can I meet Lieutenant Gobind Singh, my fiancé, please?'

He tried his best, but he couldn't hide his shock. The naval manual did not permit such a meeting. Furthermore, allowing Gobind to meet the lady could also make him an accomplice to the crime, bringing his own promising career to a grinding halt. The complex and tricky scenario he was faced with was not addressed in the rule book either. He struggled for suitable words, stammered a bit and looked at his staff, who were curiously watching the ongoing proceedings. Standing on the submarine deck to receive his commanding officer, the XO was sharp enough to sense the brewing trouble. He sprang into action and jumped on to the gangway. Manoeuvring through the steel wires of the truck-mounted crane stationed at the jetty to lift the gangway before the submarine's cast off, he ran through the steps, saluted and stood next to his CO.

Without responding to the salute, the CO whispered into his ears. The XO nodded. 'Let me handle this, sir,' he said. In a swift motion, he pulled out his walkie-talkie from his waist belt and passed the orders, 'The Hon'ble Defence Minister wishes to meet Lieutenant Gobind Singh,' and waited for a response. A moment later, he nodded and turned towards the CO. 'He will be here soon, sir.'

'Thank you,' the captain acknowledged and turned towards the minister while responding to Taraa. 'Sir, as desired by you, Lieutenant Gobind Singh would be here soon.' The minister smiled and looked at Taraa, who clenched both her hands into fists in excitement. Getting closer to her father, she exclaimed with joy and cheer. 'O thank you so much, Papa. I am so very grateful.'

Both the father and the minister smiled back at her. 'Thank you, captain,' said the minister. 'I am sorry for this inconvenience, but it has been brought to my notice that a wrong perception has been created about one of your officers for some selfish and petty reasons. Therefore, I decided to clear the air before you set sail, even if it meant bending a few rules here and there.' Saying this, the minister began walking towards the stern of the submarine. Karamanov and Captain Raju followed, but Taraa stayed put. Her eyes were focused on the periscope bridge, expecting Gobind to emerge from the chimney-shaped like black hooded structure on top of the submarine.

A minute or so later, a flabbergasted Gobind came out of the open hatch on the deck instead and looked at the commander. Following the XO's hand that pointed towards the lady in a gown, his eyes locked on to Taraa's. Having already changed into battle rig, Gobind hesitated at first. But after taking a go-ahead from his immediate boss, he climbed on the gangway one step at a time, as if he was walking through a mine field. He had now become the centre of attention for the entire crowd assembled on the jetty. The periscope bridge too was filled to the brim with officers jostling for the right spot to witness the rendezvous of the modern day Romeo and Juliet.

He stepped down and hesitatingly moved towards Taraa. Standing in front of her, he looked around and realized that people were slowly beginning to cheer. He held her hand and pressed it gently and whispered. 'Only

my Taraa could have done this.' She smiled happily, swung the hat off her head with one flick, and stepping forward, she hugged him and wrapped her arms around his neck like a garland. The hat caught the wind and flew off over the spectators, turning the audience's gentle cheer into a rousing cheer. Embarrassed by the applause, she buried her head deep into Gobind's chest and spoke without looking up. 'I told you that my Papa will sort this man out, didn't I? And now, you may kiss your bride.' Before Gobind could even react, she stood up on her toes and planted her lips on Gobind's.

The applause grew louder and almost turned into a frenzy. As the crowd jostled and inched closer, Dimitrinov turned back and briskly moved towards his black limousine. He sat in his car in a hurry and sped away. Emboldened by the XO's happy face, the crew on the periscope deck too joined in and started shouting 'Taraa! Taraa! Taraa!' She looked up, saw Muthu, and waved. 'Thank you, Muthu!' she screamed gleefully while still staying close to Gobind. Meanwhile, the minister, Karamanov, and the captain came back.

Gobind parted company but not without another hug. 'Look after yourself,' he said. 'I will miss you.' Then, turning towards his CO, he respectfully said, 'Sir, I have the honour of introducing you to my fiancé, soon to become Taraa Gobind Singh.' Caught in an awkward position, the CO meekly smiled back and bowed slightly. 'Thank you, Ma'am. Welcome to the family,' he said and looked at his watch, sending a signal to Gobind that it was getting

late. Simultaneously, he turned towards the minister and saluted. 'Request permission to cast off, sir.'

'Permission granted. Have a safe journey ahead,' came a crisp, diplomatic reply from the Russian minister.

Gobind nodded and thanked Karamanov and the Minister before jumping on to the gangway and to the *Sindhkosh* deck. The last man to arrive on board, the CO stood in attention on the deck and saluted while a hundred flags waived. '*Dasvidaniya!*' the crowd screamed loudly.

On the edge of the jetty, Taraa stood alone, waving till the shark-shaped, long, black tube, ceremoniously covered with ensigns from forecastle to quarterdeck, sailed past the horizon.

19

Sitting in the Combat Information Centre (CIC), the nerve centre of the submarine, Captain Raju looked into the monitors in front as the *Sindhkosh* continued on its maiden passage to India. His right-hand man, Commander Adish Behramji, the XO, stood by his side while the officer of the watch (OOW), controlled the direction, speed, depth and a wide range of colourful instruments that were blinking their presence.

The steward came and stood next to the captain's chair. Without glancing towards him, the CO said, 'One please.' 'Same for me,' said the XO. Putting one cube of sugar in each cup, the steward handed over the tea mugs to both the officers and left.

'Sir, I see that you're quite disturbed by the turn of events that took place prior to our casting off. Would you like to discuss it? I think you should get it out of your system.'

The CO looked at the XO and placed the tea cup on top of the gyro repeater, partially covering the OOW's ability to view the exact direction *Sindhkosh* was headed to. But he didn't bother. The sea was fairly calm for the waves to force any change in the submarine's direction. The tea mug clattered slightly as the gyro moved on its swivel, but its noise was too feeble in comparison to the storm that was brewing and threatening to burst inside the captain's mind. Holding on to the hand bar on the bulk head, he turned sideways towards the XO. 'Am I glad you raised this issue, Adish! Frankly, I am indeed disturbed.'

As if the XO was anticipating the next scene to unfold, he nodded and inched closer. The CO continued. 'For whatever reasons, every protocol has been broken by *Sindhkosh* at Leningrad. We have actually become a laughing stock in the eyes of the world. What was supposed to be a secret affair in this voyage has actually turned into some freak Laila-Majnu show. We shall be hogging all the headlines tomorrow in every Russian newspaper. The entire town will know that we have set off for Bombay. I am sure the report will reach the naval headquarters well before we touch the Indian shores. Be prepared to answer some tough questions. The top brass is going to make mincemeat out of us.' Having let go off his frustration, Captain Raju turned back towards the array of brightly lit multicoloured instruments in front, but his mind was still at the Leningrad jetty.

Adish held the mug in his hand but didn't drink from it. Instead, he kept stirring it with the small teaspoon

submerged in it. The faint smile on his face didn't go unnoticed and perturbed the CO.' Is there something funny, Adish?'

Not to be easily caught off guard, the XO was quick to respond. 'Sir, I feel we are overreacting a bit. In my humble submission, there is a second view point. Gobind fell in love with this beautiful girl who belongs to an affluent family. It has happened before, and it shall happen again. A villain steps in and pushes his luck, but the hero finally emerges triumphant. It's a simple Hindi blockbuster film with a mixed Russian cast. What Gobind doesn't know yet is that he still has an uphill task ahead. Our cumbersome, red-tape entrenched bureaucratic system will not permit him to walk away easily. I guess he'll have to choose between a career in the Indian Navy and his Russian bride.'

The CO wasn't impressed by his XO's philosophical response. In an irritated voice, he cut in between. 'We are talking about a few careers that could face the heat. I have much more experience than you, and I am aware of how the NHQ will react. What the hell was I doing? They'll ask. What was the XO up to? They'll want to know. Be prepared to receive some below the-belt punches as well. They dip their pens in acid on the slightest provocation while writing our Annual Confidential Report (ACR). Given the navy's damn narrow pyramid structure, we'll be lucky if the sharks at NHQ let us get away with this open display of romance.' Worried by the consequences of the possible adverse question marks on his leadership qualities, the CO had completely forgotten about the tea mug lying

on the gyro repeater, and as a courtesy, the XO didn't consume his tea either.

'I do appreciate your concern, sir,' continued the XO. 'Situations can either make you bitter or better. Cursing a flat tyre won't fix it. Let's brainstorm on this while we have time. I am sure there'll be an opportunity.'

Having made his point, the XO waited for the CO to respond. Instead, the captain stood up from his chair and, without looking at the XO, headed for his cabin. 'Maintain the course, speed and depth, OOW. Call me whenever in doubt.'

'Aye, aye, sir', replied the duty officer and took position behind the gyro repeater as soon as the mug was removed.

As night fell, the Middle Watch closed up. *Sindhkosh* was doing slow ahead on its main motor, cruising at a depth of 100 metres below sea level. Lt Gobind Singh took over as the officer on watch and began his duty by diligently noting readings on various panels and keeping a sharp eye on all the instruments. Barely fifteen minutes into his duty, the control room raised a frantic alarm: 'FLOODING, FLOODING, FLOODING.' Picking up the intercom in one swift move, Gobind inquired, 'What happened?'

'Sir, there has been a major rupture on the sea water pipe. The main ballast pump has given way. Water is gushing in rapidly at over a 10-kg pressure!' came an urgent response. Gobind rang the alarm, closed up 'Action Stations' by broadcasting on the central speakers and simultaneously informed the captain. The CO tried to rush to the CIC but found himself locked in his compartment.

'Why's my compartment sealed, Gobind?' he demanded on the sound-powered telephones as the intercoms too had stopped functioning due to the power failure.

'Sir, the rapid ingress of water requires the immediate isolation of the control room from the rest of the submarine in order to stop the spread of flooding to other compartments. The forward compartment hatch is sealed to protect torpedoes, missiles and batteries, and the officers' cabins being in the same space have got isolated automatically.'

'Oh, okay. You will have to handle this by yourself. Keep me posted every minute.'

'Aye, aye, sir,' replied Gobind and began to put into action what was taught to him during comprehensive training in Russia. 'Shut down all hull valves exposed to sea water,' he ordered and told the planesman to give a maximum up angle to the planes.

'Full ahead,' he ordered, hoping to be able to surface and thereby reduce the pressure of ingress of water. But the flow of water was so intense at that depth that the control-room hold was soon flooded. The bilge pump too reported malfunctioning. All other ballast pumps were switched on and put into action. The water ingress also resulted in partial power failure. Auto voltage regulators began sparking and had to be shut down to prevent a fire break out. The submarine was soon reduced to using emergency lighting.

The rapidity of the flooding was causing the submarine to gain depth with every passing moment because of the

additional weight of the water. Gobind tried his best to create an up angle to steady the boat at its scheduled depth. Two crew personnel who tried to access the damaged area suffered injuries due to the force of water gushing into the submarine, throwing them back against the bulkhead. The traditional physical damage control measures had become ineffective against the water gushing in at a rapid pace.

Showing remarkable control and composure, Gobind kept the CO's communications system on, allowing him to constantly monitor every activity at the CIC. He simultaneously ordered an emergency surfacing procedure (ESP) by blowing the ballast, hoping and silently praying that the submarine's high pressure air system would function to its potential. However, the boat kept going down; the depth metre indicating 175 metres, which only kept increasing. 'Sir, we can't let her go below 225 metres. It'll hit the bottom,' panicked the planesman.

Gobind's heart was thumping wildly. Yet, he was displaying a positive attitude and not letting his anxiety become obvious to the crew, a trait that had been drilled into him during numerous emergency training drills. The calmness in his voice while passing orders was remarkable for an officer of his age and limited experience. Consequently, it had a soothing effect on the crew and kept hopes alive.

All eyes in the CIC were fixed on the depth gauge and the echo sounder but the latter too began indicating erratic figures. As the boat crossed 190 metres, he felt the descent was slowing. The experienced planesman was doing his very best to keep the submarine on level. Gobind's thoughts

fleetingly went to his family and Taraa. A silent prayer crossed his lips, '*De Shiva var mohe eha . . .*'

However, soon, the depth-gauge needle began moving dangerously towards the crushing depth mark and the panicking plainsman kept shouting, '195 . . . 200 . . . 205 . . . 210.' But, suddenly, his commentary halted. The depth metre reading panel flickered for a couple of seconds and then, to everyone's great relief, began moving upwards. The planesman began screaming in excitement, '209 . . . 207 . . . 205 . . . 202 . . . 197. Sir, she's going up.' The effect of blowing the ballast in emergency had begun to take effect and the boat began to surface rapidly. Gobind kept his calm despite the panic-ridden faces all around and continued to carry out the drill to perfection. The steadiness in his voice had a positive effect on his emergency team as the submarine kept gaining ground till it almost bounced on to the surface. Amidst a collective sigh of relief in the control room and among the rest of the crew on board, he rapidly passed orders for immediate repairs to the damaged pipes and ballast pumps and rushed the technical teams for damage control.

Then, Gobind turned his attention to pumping out the sea water and ordered opening of the forward compartment, letting the captain get an access to the CIC. At the same time, he ordered medical help for the two injured sailors. The crew responded at an exemplary pace and moved the injured sailors to the sickbay. A glance at the clock showed that what seemed a lifetime had been less than ten minutes. The CO rushed into the CIC and found Gobind

in complete control of the situation and rattling orders in quick succession like a seasoned campaigner. His voice was as composed as was his methodical, deft handling of the emergency. With admiration-filled eyes, the captain stood at the CIC entrance and waited patiently as the young lieutenant addressed the crew on the central broadcast system.

'Do you hear there? Do you hear there? This is the officer of the watch speaking. We have just emerged from an emergency. Each department is to immediately carry out an inspection of all equipment, ballast tank valves and pressure pipes and report status to CIC. All officers to stay at their duty stations till further orders. Electrical department to restore main power. Batteries to be put on charge. *Sindhkosh* to stay in action stations until further orders.'

Standing bare feet in shorts and a vest that had torn off in places while rushing to the CIC, Captain Sundaram Raju was awestruck by his young officer's raw courage, high professionalism and meticulous handling of an extreme situation while remaining remarkably calm. Not even in his wildest dreams had he ever thought of Gobind to be possessing such abilities. Placing the receiver on the hook, Gobind turned back to find the CO standing in front. 'Good evening, sir,' he greeted.' All in control.'

An overwhelmed captain let go off his emotions. His ego balloon had been busted. Deeply humbled by the innocent-looking brave heart's tremendous actions, he stepped forward and put his hand of Gobind's shoulder

and smiled even as his eyes were filled with gratitude. 'You're a gem, son. You have just saved us all from a watery grave. I am extremely sorry for my rude behaviour. Go to the periscope deck and catch some fresh air. I have her for now. And, you must know that I am proud of you.'

Gobind smiled back and saluted smartly. Even if the CO was taking over the watch, there was a drill that had to be mandatorily completed. Placing his notebook on the gyro repeater, he said, 'Aye, aye, sir. All hands are on action stations; sea water valves are shut. Power is being restored. Batteries are being put on charge. All parameters are within limits, and temperatures are in control. Mains switched off till further orders from CIC and ballast tanks are fully operational. *Sindhkosh* is on surface, sailing at a speed of 10 knots on its pre-set direction. Request permission to leave the CIC, sir.'

Captain Raju was left speechless and overwhelmed to witness the calm and composed face of an officer, rattling out handing over duties drill despite having gone through a traumatic, life-threatening emergency. 'Thank you, Gobind. I have her,' he managed to acknowledge. Stretching slightly, he picked up the note book from the repeater to take a look at the recordings.

As Gobind stepped out of the CIC, he heard the CO passing orders to the chief quartermaster. 'Maintain course and speed.' The CO then spoke on the internal broadcast, 'This in the captain speaking. All sections to report parameters status ASAP,' and began recording notes in the log book by himself.

Gobind stepped out and ran into the XO. Before he could wish him, the XO's words poured out. 'Bravo, Zulu young man,' he exclaimed with joy. 'You've proven today what only I always knew. My personal gratitude too. It happens to be my birthday today and you've given me the biggest gift ever, a new lease of life!'

'Oh. Many happy returns of the day, sir. Wish you a long and happy life ahead.'

'Thanks. Go and get fresh air. You've done more than your share already,' said the XO with a relieved face and entered the CIC.

20

INS *Sindhkosh* was towed into the inner side of the South breakwater jetty at the Bombay dockyard. Two small, but powerful tugs pushed and nudged it gently to secure it alongside. New and brightly shining yellow intertwined thick nylon ropes run across the submarine deck to the bollards, securing it firmly alongside. Dot on time, the fleet commander's car drove through the long and narrow jetty amidst the sound of alert pipes from the war ships in the vicinity. The admiral stepped down from his car to inspect the latest addition of deadly weaponry to the Western Fleet's war arsenal. Smartly dressed in a formal white uniform, Captain Sundaram Raju was standing on the deck to welcome the Fleet Commander, Rear Admiral Bhaskar Rao, on board with complete ceremonials. Four quartermasters manned the gangway in attention on board the freshly touched up black solid steel deck.

The admiral acknowledged salutes and took a firm grip on the admiralty pattern gold-brass studded ceremonial sword in his left hand. He stepped on the gangway and waited for a brief moment, allowing the duty officer to commence the ceremony. On a cue, the OOD shouted, 'Standby to pipe.' The quartermasters lifted the pipes to their mouths and took a deep breath. The admiral began his slow, measured march forward. It's important for the duty officer to shout the word 'pipe' at the perfect time. It is mandatory in the navy for the quartermasters to begin and end blowing the musical pipes in one single breath within which VIPs must reach the warship deck. If it ends even a little before or after, it is considered as a wrong drill and speaks poorly of both the crew and the CO.

The admiral walked without holding the side rails just to display his physical fitness and mental agility. As he reached the half-way mark, a distance far enough for the quartermasters to take a deep breath in anticipation, the duty officer orders, 'Pipe.' In unison, the four quartermasters blew the longish thin whistle. Its thin and sharp sound travelled across the jetty. Everyone on the deck and in the vicinity came to a standstill while the commanding officer and his men on board raised their right arm to salute.

The admiral halted briefly at the edge of the gangway, acknowledged the salutes by saluting back and stepped on to the deck in a short and swift move. Pleased by his own successful acrobatics, he looks at the CO with a broad smile on his face. 'Welcome home, Raju. Well done and congratulations.'

The CO stepped closer, shook hands and put on his best smiling face. 'Thank you, sir. Welcome on board *Sindhkosh*, your latest underwater weapon, sir.'

The admiral glanced at the officers on the deck, shook hands with them and turned towards the CO. 'I believe it was quite a close shave. Fantastic work by your crew. I am so relieved and proud to see my fighting fit unit safe and sound. If you'll recall, each officer was personally handpicked by me.'

It wasn't lost on the CO that the beaming fleet commander was fishing for compliments. He nodded his head vigorously in affirmation as if his life was depending upon the speed at which his neck swung up and down. Standing by his side, Commander Adish Behramji, the XO too joined in agreement but with a single nod. 'We are indeed thankful to you, sir, for putting us all together as a team,' said the CO in a tone that appeared like the icing on a cake.

The admiral looked at him thoughtfully and suddenly became serious. 'I have one regret though, Raju. I made a mistake in shortlisting Lt Gobind Singh. Where's he? His misconduct put me in a great deal of embarrassment. Signals are flying left and right seeking explanations. Since the complaint against him has come directly from the NHQ, I was left with no choice but to order a Board of Inquiry (BOI). If found guilty, he shall have to face a court martial. He looked promising to me. But then, we are not perfect after all, are we?'

The admiral looked at the CO for his reaction and noticed that the captain and the XO both looked shocked.

Captain Raju's consistent head movement also came to a grinding halt as if emergency brakes had been applied on it.

Reacting instantly, the admiral demanded, 'Why this strange reaction captain? What's bitten you?'

'Sir, may I humbly request not to rush into this BOI? Had it not been for Gobind, *Sindhkosh* would have been sitting in Davy Jones' locker with all hands on board. His competence, presence of mind, intelligence and fearlessness has saved the day for us. I too had a wrong impression about him. However, after this incident at sea, I realized that he is an important asset for the Indian Navy. Any harm to his career at this stage would mean a big blow to the submarine arm and the nation. May I request you to reconsider your decision, sir?'

The CO looked at his XO who instantly jumped in seconding his captain. 'Sir,' began the XO, stepping forward, 'exercising emergency drills in peaceful waters is one thing. But performing them on board in a war-like situation so professionally while maintaining composure, and that too in not-so-calm seas, is quite another. At one stage, we had all given up hope. But Gobind stood his ground. His hands-on knowledge of emergency procedures and drills, a knowhow of intricate technology and expertise on ballast tanks operations are simply outstanding. Using alternate power supply, he singlehandedly surfaced *Sindhkosh* from the near crushing 200 metres' depth in quick time. He deserves to be commended for the highest honour and definitely not be belittled with a BOI.'

'Oh, is that so?' exclaimed the admiral. 'Why didn't you make a comprehensive signal to this effect? What do we do now? I have already ordered the BOI.' Realizing his fault, the admiral's left hand shook a little as a result of which the bottom tip of his ceremonial sword cover hit the metal deck, emitting a thin metallic sound. The four quartermasters remained in attention posture whilst overhearing the conversation. That their sympathies were with Lt Gobind Singh was well visible from their painful facial reactions.

The CO responded immediately in a slow but clear tone. 'Sir, there was a strict restriction on signal traffic. Besides, I was scheduled to brief you on return. And I had no idea of the NHQ orders.'

Stunned silence prevailed while the admiral began to think about it. He walked towards the forecastle, the CO and XO following him in a single line formation. Manoeuvring through the narrow pathway while crossing the fin, the admiral turned his head sideways and glanced at the captain. 'Written orders, once issued under copy to the NHQ, have to be mandatorily complied with. And given the regulations of the Indian Navy (regs navy) guidelines, it would be difficult for Gobind to find an escape route from the vice-like grip of the legal arm. I don't see any hope.'

As soon as the admiral reached the open forecastle, he began pacing up and down on the long and curvy narrow deck. Both the officers struggled to keep up with him while ensuring to maintain reasonable distance. His pace was erratic and his free walk hampered by thick nylon ropes

running across the deck. And then, all of a sudden, the admiral snapped his fingers. 'I have an idea. It's possible to wind up the BOI. Where's Gobind? Call him.'

The duty officer's ears and eyes were tuned to listening to any order being passed. Without waiting for his CO's directives, he rushed to the central announcement system and withdrew a tiny water proof instrument neatly stuck into the bulkhead cavity. Swiftly, he switched it on by pressing it gently and announced on the internal broadcast: 'Lt Gobind Singh requested at the gangway by the fleet commander.' By the time he pushed the instrument back into the cavity, the below-deck hatch swung open upwards amidst the crackling sound of the functioning levers. A sparkling white turban appeared first, followed by the full figure of Lt Gobind Singh. He looked perplexed but rushed to the forecastle and smartly saluted the admiral.

'Good morning, Gobind,' the admiral greeted him with a smile.

'Jai Hind, sir', came Gobind's instant response, with the palm of his right hand facing towards his right eye. The salute was near perfect. The words *Jai Hind* were spoken with equal perfection.

'I had received a formal written complaint about your misconduct on foreign soil, which forced me to order a BOI. But your CO has just brought to my attention your commendable act at sea wherein you have single handedly saved *Sindhkosh* and all the lives on board it. He has therefore strongly recommended the command to reconsider its decision. But having already ordered the

BOI, the only option left is that you plead not guilty and deny the charges of your affair with this Russian girl. And we shall find a way to close the BOI.' Finishing his short speech, the admiral looked triumphantly towards the CO and XO. While the captain's head resumed its up and down movement, the XO didn't look quite convinced.

'Sir, thank you so much for your kindness. I am grateful. But, sir, I cannot lie about my relationship with Taraa. She's my fiancée, sir.'

Gobind's brief and crisp reply didn't go well with the admiral. His so-called brilliant escape route for the young officer stood shattered. More so, he was visibly shaken and taken aback by a junior officer's point-blank negative response. He almost thundered in anger, his voice travelling to the length and breadth of *Sindhkosh*. 'What? Fiancée? Do you know that contact with foreign nationals by a service officer is a serious offence? What happened in Russia is done and over with. You have an opportunity to make a new beginning. The Indian Navy doesn't want to lose a brilliant officer. But you'll have to promise to let go off your past. Is that clear?' As a result, a host of officers and sailors standing on the deck and the jetty stayed at attention, curiously waiting for the outcome of arguments between an admiral and a young lieutenant.

'Sir,' Gobind began, 'I humbly state that back home, in Bihar, my mother taught me to always stick to the truth. And the fact is that I cannot deny the existence of Taraa Karamanov, a Russian national, in my life. I also cannot lie that we're not in love. It's a fact that we have got engaged

at the Hare Krishna temple. I shall not get married without prior permission from the command. But I shall not lie, under oath or otherwise, about my relationship with Taraa. I reaffirm and am willing to assure under oath that at no point of time did I ever discuss anything related to the project or my job with anyone outside my immediate submarine crew . . .'

Before Gobind could even conclude, a frustrated and angry admiral stepped back and turned towards the commanding officer. The captain looked petrified by the consequences of a young lieutenant standing firm against the wishes of the fleet commander. But a calm and composed XO stood at ease, evaluating the developments. The gangway staff too wore fearful looks on their faces and stood motionlessly. In his thirty years of service, the chief quartermaster had never witnessed anything like that. His eyes reflected amazement, fear and respect for the youngest officer on board.

'So, BOI it is then, captain. I expected better communication standards on board your sub. This is utter nonsense. I dare say that the level of discipline on board *Sindhkosh* is, at best, pathetic. I am unhappy. Negative Bravo Zulu.' Fuming and murmuring expletives, he turned to his left to momentarily glance one last time at Gobind and walked towards the gangway. The CO rushed to man the station. Anticipating his departure, the XO ordered, 'Standby to pipe.' The four quartermasters quickly bent their right arms at their elbows and held the pipes in between their lips. And as the admiral stood on the gangway, the

XO completed the ceremony like a seasoned campaigner. The CO stood frozen on the deck, fully aware that he could no longer expect any more golden stripes to be added on his shoulders. The admiral's comment, 'Negative Bravo Zulu' had summarily ended his future career prospects.

All movements on the jetty came to a grinding halt yet again as the fleet commander's entourage sped away, leaving behind a sulking CO and stunned officers. Not too far away, the tug master let go off a long hooter. The propellers began churning rapidly, displacing a large volume of water in their wake. The waves formed as a consequence hit the first closest object, the Sindhkosh, shaking it from its hull and causing a strong yaw-yaw movement on the submarine. Standing with an upset mind and without support, the CO was caught off balance. However, before he could fall, Gobind held his hand with a firm grip and helped him regain his balance. The captain looked into Gobind's eyes and broke into a smile. 'Son, I admire your courage. Your bravery and will power are petrifying and admirable at the same time. I want you to know that I shall be recommending your name for the second highest gallantry award, the Veer Chakra.'

The captain saw no excitement in Gobind after hearing the news. Surprised, he continued, 'You don't look happy. In the armed forces, our men and officers make supreme sacrifices, yet don't get considered for a gallantry award. I am amazed to see no reaction from you. Is everything okay?'

Gobind smiled and came to attention. 'Sir, my mother says that if the Lord grants you karma, then that itself is an

award. There cannot be anything bigger than that. I feel blessed to be able to save the *Sindhkosh*. That feeling is so unique and pure. I don't wish for anything else. But I am thankful to you for your encouraging words.'

The CO looked at his young officer in admiration. 'Hats off to your mother. May God bless you,' he spoke softly and stepped down the ladder. The XO came next and looked into his eyes. A thin smile spread across his face as he did so. He put his left hand on Gobind's shoulder and said, 'You're a brave son of Bihar. I am sure you'll emerge stronger from these incidents. Keep it up.' Without waiting for a response, he too followed his CO to the compartments below.

Left alone, Gobind went closer to the guardrails and looked at the waves that were still hitting the submarine hull at regular intervals. The sound of moving boots hitting the steel deck made him turn around to find the chief quartermaster approaching him. He stood face to face at an arm's length, saluted and paused before speaking. 'Sir, may I humbly request you to grace the occasion of my daughter's wedding by your kind presence this Sunday? Without you, I wouldn't have been able to perform my karma.'

Gobind saluted back and looked visibly pleased to hear the news. He stepped forward and shook hands with him. 'I will, Master Sahib. Heartiest congratulations.' But the senior sailor wasn't done yet. 'Sir, right from my childhood, I was taught that one should live with great memories and not just dreams. I have learnt its true meaning today. And I now also realize why Subedar Bhawani Singh held you in

such high esteem. It's a privilege to be working with you, sir. Thank you so much. Jai Hind.'

The mention of Bhawani Singh's name brought a big smile on Gobind's face, helping him momentarily forget the brewing tensions. Adjusting his white turban with both hands, he asked, 'How do you know him Master Sahib?'

The master chief promptly replied. 'Sir, Bhawani retired as an honorary captain recently. It's his son, a marine engineer, who is getting married to my daughter. However, I humbly request you to please attend the wedding from the girl's side. As goes the naval tradition, we're all one big family on board. I, therefore, have more rights than Bhawani.'

An overwhelmed Gobind nodded, shook hands again and politely said. 'Indeed we're a family, Master Sahib. As you wish. I would like to share with you that the Honorary Captain Bhawani Singh was not just an instructor. He was also my guru. Had it not been for his tough training and strict discipline, I wouldn't have been standing on board *Sindhkosh* today. It shall be my honour to be at the ceremony in August.' The master chief was awestruck to hear the young lieutenant's sentiments for a retired instructor. He saw him enter the open hatch and stepping down the ladder into the decks below. 'We are all proud of you, sir,' he said to himself and saluted again even as Lt Gobind Singh wasn't in listening range. With pride in his eyes, he returned to the gangway to find the other quartermasters nodding their heads in agreement. Entering the hatch, Gobind released the steel bars and landed firmly on him

feet at the deck below, and he saw Muthu waiting for him. 'Welcome, Mr James Bond. It's my duty to inform you that we are no longer in Leningrad and you're not the 007. So, please learn to hold your horses.' And the two friends hugged each other.

21

The Western Naval Command Officer's Mess at Navy Nagar, Colaba, arguably offered one of the most beautiful and picturesque landscapes in Bombay. Located on the banks of the vast, blue Arabian Sea, it is like a paradise isolated from the metropolitan concrete jungle. It's surrounded by an abundant lush green cover, flora and fauna. Tall palm trees, colourful flower beds, neatly manured grass on the beautifully maintained golf course, and a 2-kilometre-long walking track add to its breathtaking view. It ushers in a peaceful, stress-busting environment to any tired mind. Every evening, the setting sun's bright reddish-orange hue offers a sight that is a delight to any photographer's lens and is worth taking a 100-mile journey.

As the sun sinks into the gigantic ocean every evening, its pristine, serene and scenic beauty absorbs one's worries and tensions and leaves behind a fully charged-up body to take on challenges afresh the next day.

The Indian Navy on its part ensured that the cantonment stayed immaculately clean, pollution free and calm. Unlike the super-rich municipal corporation of India's financial capital, everything that is required to function simply performs to its optimum capacity, at a bare-minimum cost.

But a sudden movement of scores of red beaconed, siren-hooting cars changed that scenario one fine morning, forcing heads to turn in disbelief. The ensuing hustle and bustle at the command mess had already set the rumour mills running. All eyes were focused on the board room that was abuzz with hushed conversations. Descending from their respective cars, a host of senior officers were escorted into the hall and seated around a large, rectangle-shaped wooden table. Each chair was marked and labelled with the name of its occupant by a placard.

Being part of the Board of Inquiry (BOI) ordered by the Western Naval Command (WNC) Headquarters, their primary assignment was to investigate Lt Gobind Singh's unauthorized contact with foreign nationals whilst on a secret mission to Russia and provide a suitable course of action to the fleet commander. Lying on the table in front of every officer were the thick, blue volumes of the regs navy, also known as the bible governing the rules and regulations of the Indian Navy.

Rear Admiral Suryavansh Thapar, the senior-most officer and thereby the chairman of the BOI was busy flipping pages and making notes when Lt Gobind Singh was ushered into the room. Seated on Admiral Thapar's right was Commodore Bhanushali, the former boss of Lt

Gobind Singh. From the expression on his face, it was evident that the commodore was not quite happy with the proceedings ordered against a bright and promising officer, but due to the service's demands, he kept his feelings to himself.

Gobind stood in front of the admiral, saluted and waited for instructions. The calm and peace on his face did not show any reflection of fear or anxiety that he might have been harbouring within. 'Please sit down, Gobind,' came a polite command. Gobind did as directed and looked over the row of brightly shining golden stripes on the shoulders of the officers seated in front. The vast, deep sea across the big windows at the back looked calm, majestic and soothing. Admiral Thapar was quick to follow Gobind's eyes. Glancing back briefly, he spoke in a soft but firm tone.

'Lt Gobind Singh, under the various articles of the regs navy, as placed in front of you, you have been charged with the following offences:

Of wilfully coming into contact with foreign nationals
Of getting engaged to a foreign national without prior permission from higher authorities
Of passing on information about the Indian Navy's mission in Leningrad to this particular foreign national
Of causing embarrassment to Captain Sundaram Raju prior to sailing from Leningrad port
Of causing embarrassment to the fleet commander in front of naval personnel on board INS *Sindhkosh*

Do you plead guilty?'

There was a hushed silence in the room. The big round clock on the wall ticked, one second at a time, breaking the silence code each passing moment. Sitting in an attentive posture, Gobind looked straight at the admiral but didn't respond, forcing the BOI chairman to repeat the question.

'Lt Gobind Singh, do you plead guilty?'

This time, the admiral stressed on his name a bit more as if attempting to give him a shakeup.

Gobind stayed calm, kept his head steady and replied in soft but firm voice. 'Not guilty, sir.'

'And what's your defence, Lieutenant?' countered the admiral while the steno typist ran his fingers rapidly on the typewriter.

'Sir, I humbly state that nowhere in the regs navy it is mentioned that while on a foreign mission, working and interacting with foreigners on a daily basis, the Indian Navy personnel cannot meet and exchange pleasantries with the foreign nationals. Quite often, the social functions hosted for or by the Indian Navy overseas are attended by foreigners only. Is every officer attending official functions overseas investigated?'

The admiral looked sideways, poured water from a bottle and took a sip before proceeding. 'You are not being questioned for attending functions, Lt Gobind Singh. You're being charged for acts of treason, of wilfully meeting a foreign national and maintaining a relationship without the knowledge or prior written permission of the

naval command. These are serious charges. What do you have to say in your defence?'

'Sir, I have the honour to submit that any charge without proof has no merit. I fully understand my responsibilities and duties. I am also sure that I have performed every assigned task to the best of my abilities and with a great degree of success. Labelling me with such heinous charges belittles and humiliates me. If there's even a single proof supporting any of the charges of treason, I shall willingly accept the strictest punishment.'

'Don't you think that the authorities would have done due diligence before ordering a BOI?' Gobind maintained remarkable poise while listening to the admiral's barrage of questions. He glanced at all the officers sitting on the left and right of the chairman and then made eye-to-eye contact with Commodore Bhanushali.

With a confident look on his face, he replied, 'Sir, may I humbly submit that's what the BOI should investigate? Is it possible that there's a mistake or a bruised ego for which I am being made a scapegoat?'

Stunned by the young officer's bold response, the board officers reacted as if they were struck by lightning. They looked at each other, wide eyed. They were all mature and seasoned officers, yet they were taken aback by the young officer's strong and provoking response.

Recovering quickly, and without losing his composure, the admiral rephrased the question.

'Do you think, lieutenant, there's merit in the charges framed against you?'

Before the admiral's question could fill the air, Gobind's flat and short response came in.

'No, sir.'

The Admiral continued. 'Do you have any proof to substantiate your answer? Aren't you being a bit head strong and aggressive?'

Gobind shifted just a bit in his chair but kept looking into the eyes of the BOI chairman.

'Sir, the first thing I learnt, which has become a lifelong lesson for me, is that in case of a fire, one must run towards and not away from the fire. If you don't douse it, then everyone suffers. And this is the most vital aspect in every part of our general life as well. I have responded by a counter question, sir, because I needed to address your query head on and not leave it to individual interpretation. Sir, may I humbly request to be informed if the command has provided any proof, whatsoever, to substantiate the serious charges filed against me?'

The counter charge again took everyone by surprise and shocked them out their wits. The steno typists' fingers froze on the machine. He looked at the admiral and then at the officers and noticed the stupefied looks on their faces. Commodore Bhanushali kept fiddling with the paper weight, while other officers found it difficult to speak lest they be caught on the wrong foot, given the fact that every spoken word was being recorded. The admiral finally broke the silence but not before observing the complete silence amongst his board of officers.

'No. But we have sufficient circumstantial evidence, Lieutenant; thus, this inquiry to establish the truth,' replied the admiral, secretly admiring the gutsy response. He had served the navy long enough to filter facts from fiction, knew deep within that Gobind was not entirely at fault. But he had an assigned task on hand and a duty to perform. Glancing at his notes briefly, he decided to switch to a more rational approach and ease up the rising tension in the board room.

'Can you please explain what according to you are the facts of the case?' The pen held in between his fingers spun and slipped out. It rolled on the table making a loud swirling noise, breaking the serious expressions of officers at the long table. Retrieving it quickly, the admiral hooked it over the file cover and placed both his hands below his chin. 'Ah,' he said, 'please go ahead.'

'Sir, I met Ms Taraa Karamanov at a joint naval function in Leningrad. We fell in love. Much later, I learnt that her father was amongst the richest businessmen in Moscow. Another Russian businessman, who apparently wanted his son to marry Taraa, tried to push me out of the equation by floating the honey-trap theory. The Russian government realized the mischief and gracefully admitted to it. None other than the Russian defence minister came calling prior to *Sindhkosh* setting sails for India. The clarifications issued by him are on record. Unfortunately, however, our archaic system found it difficult to let go, and our bureaucracy doesn't miss any opportunity to downgrade our forces. It is painfully true that we use

words like board of inquiry or court martial, which are like harassment for any serving officer, just to display our superiority or massage our bruised egos, sir.'

'Were you not aware that meeting a lady outside of the work space is not permitted as per the regs navy?'

'Sir, I fell in love with her. Regs navy does not bar me from that. It restricts me from discussing my business and project details. Ms Karamanov was my tour guide as well. In my capacity, I did due diligence before going around with her. She is the daughter of a highly respected gentleman who has no interest or business in armaments. If I have made a mistake, I am willing to accept any punishment this august BOI assigns, sir.'

The admiral pondered Gobind's statement for a while before continuing. 'Do you realize that your career could be over if you stick to your decision of marrying the lady in question because it is against the basic tenets of the naval laws? Why do you wish to invite trouble?'

Gobind's head turned slowly, carefully observing the faces of all the officers sitting in front. He weighed his words carefully before responding. 'Sir, I beg to submit that nothing in this world is permanent, not even our troubles. I have failed in love once and suffered immensely. I shall not let that happen again. The fire inside me is burning brighter than the fire around me. My love for Taraa is as pure as the soul within. I am determined to marry her but shall seek permission before taking the plunge.'

Realizing the far-reaching consequences of the acceptance of what he had done, Gobind had made,

Commodore Bhanushali decided to tone it down a bit and intervened. 'Other than fighting fire first hand, what else have you learnt officer?'

'Sir, there's one golden rule for submarining that is followed universally. It is also equally applicable to the civil world.'

'And that is?' piped in one of the officers.

'That every diving must be equal to surfacing. A submarine must surface each time it dives. I have learnt that attacking problems with equal grit is vital for surfacing as well as balancing and stabilizing one's mind.' Gobind paused briefly before continuing. 'I quote Admiral Rudolf Golosov of the Russian navy. "Submariners are a special brotherhood, either all come to the surface or no one does."'

'Lieutenant Gobind Singh, did you face indiscrimination or rude behaviour from anyone on board during your return passage, given the fact that your actions had caused embarrassment to the commanding officer?'

'Sir, I have learnt that unlike in war ships or in business, there's practically no escape from a colleague, peer or senior that one doesn't get along with. In order to bring in cohesiveness and generate a win-win situation, it is of paramount importance to resolve differences and carry on. I can say with full faith and confidence that I was not mistreated by anyone on board during our return passage or at any other point of time.'

Except for the typewriter that went on clickity-click at a steady pace, there wasn't another sound. The admiral opened the water bottle again, filled the glass almost up

to the brim and drank it slowly. The other board officers followed suit. A dozen bottles produced different sounds as the water fell into different glasses. Their eyes were glued on to Gobind, their minds evaluating every word that he was so boldly and fearlessly uttering. They were all well aware that even if they were sure about Gobind's innocence, he was well within the archaic rules of the regs navy and was, therefore, a fit candidate to be court-martialled.

Placing his glass on the table, the admiral paused and rubbed his forehead with the palm of his hand. Gobind's counter accusations going on record had put him in a bind. Taking another quick sip from the glass, he said, 'Your would-be father-in-law is such a rich and powerful person. You can simply quit the navy and join his business.' Gobind responded without even batting an eyelid. 'Sir, it's easy to choose people who have reached great heights. But I am serving an institution that shall hold me when I fall from the heights. I firmly believe that loyalty is always better than royalty. And I shall stick to that as it is my top priority.'

The officers across the long table looked at each other. One could easily make out that they were impressed by the young officer's response. But no one spoke.

'Alright,' said the Admiral. 'Please wait outside.'

'Aye, aye, sir', replied Gobind. He saluted but kept standing.

'You wish to say something, officer?'

'Yes, sir. Had it not been for Taraa and her father, I would not have succeeded in producing the proof that the genset fitted on the yet-to-be commissioned *Sindhkosh* was

an old machine that was refabricated by the contractor to make money. Thank you, sir, for giving me the opportunity. Jai Hind.'

The admiral looked shocked when he heard this. And so did the others. He emptied the glass and gently placed it back on the table. Then, pushing the chair back, he stood up and walked towards the large window facing the ocean. Following the naval customs, all the officers too stood up and waited patiently. The admiral remained silent for a considerable time, as if he was engulfed by the vastness of the blue waters of the vast Arabian Sea in front. Nothing moved except for the sound of the Remington typewriter that went about its business nonstop. He turned and looked at his team of officers. His expressions revealed his concern for both the young lieutenant and the strict rules his team was bound by. 'Well, what do you make out of all this, gentlemen?' he asked the officers.

Commodore Bhanushali, the second senior-most officer present in the room took the lead. 'Sir, in my honest opinion, it's just a case of two youngsters falling in love. Gobind has served under me. I therefore know what mettle he's made of. I did some internal inquiry before coming here. It appears that there's no merit in the charges. We're wasting our time.'

Commodore Bhanushali's open admittance of knowing Lt Gobind Singh beforehand and his strong comments in support thereon were so loaded that the rest of the board members being juniors preferred to stay quiet. It is a common fact that providing a counter opinion to

that of a senior could sometimes also be seen as an act of insubordination, which could prove harmful to one's career at a later stage.

'I think so too,' concurred the chairman. 'But we need evidence either way as also correct interpretation of the rules. Please ask for the commander-at-arms as well as the CO and the XO to be present tomorrow morning at 0900 hours. Let's hear their views as well.'

'Aye, aye, sir,' replied the commodore as the admiral walked past the saluting officers towards the exit.

The other members waited for the steno typist to leave with his typewriter to the adjacent room. And as soon as he did, the hush-hush chat began. 'What guts this man has, I say. Obviously, the fleet commander would be cheesed off with him,' said one. 'I like his confidence. The submarine commander is on an ego trip,' said the second. 'The admiral's only interested in his next promotion,' said the third.

Tea arrived. They sat down across the same table. The steno typist returned and handed over the typed sheets to the commodore. Opening the folder, he ran through the draft of proceedings, made changes at few places in green ink and returned them to the steno. 'Please type this carefully. I want no mistakes.'

'Yes, sir,' said the typist and left. 'Mark my words,' began the commodore as soon as the typist went out of sight, 'What Lt Gobind Singh has said today shall go down in the annals of the Indian Navy's history. And its time someone did that.'

The next day, both the CO and the XO arrived together. In one corner of the table sat the commander-at-arms, the legal expert, Commander James Thomas. Admiral Thapar sat at the centre of the table but let the commodore run the show. Captain Raju entered the hall first, saluted and sat down. Admiral Thapar acknowledged and looked at his deputy. Without wasting any time, Commodore Bhanushali began reading from a typed paper. 'How do you rate Lt Gobind Singh as an officer?'

At first, the CO looked uncomfortable and shifted in his chair awkwardly. Admiral Thapar was quick to spot his discomfiture. 'Please give us a clear picture, Captain, without any fear or favour,' he said and continued. 'On your answers shall depend this officer's career. We are aware how he saved *Sindhkosh* from sinking. It'll be sad if he goes down due to your silence or incorrect reporting.'

Captain Raju felt shaken up by the admiral's observation. Correcting his posture one last time, he sat upright and began. 'Sir, Lt Gobind Singh is arguably amongst the finest officers in the submarine arms today. The fact that we are all alive is only due to this young officer's amazing presence of mind, intelligence and competence. Above all, he is an honest officer with high credibility. I rate him outstanding.'

'Good,' replied the commodore. 'Do you think by any of his acts he would have compromised the safety of the submarine?'

'No, sir,' replied the CO in a firm tone. 'I did make a mistake in understanding him initially. But he proved me wrong.'

'Good. How much light can you throw on this Russian girl?'

The CO paused a little, but without showing hesitation, he briefed the board about his meeting with the Russian defence minister. Bhanushali looked at his other members and then at the CO while the commander-at-arms made notes in his log book.

'Thank you, Captain. You may go now.' The CO stood up, saluted but before walking out addressed the admiral. 'Sir, regs navy has one rule for all. But the same should not be read differently for different people.' The admiral raised his eyebrows and smiled but kept mum.

The XO entered the hall soon after and, after the rituals, he gave a similar brief to the board. But his support for Gobind was much more emphatic. He questioned the archaic laws governing the all-important issue of contact with foreign nationals, especially when the crew was on a mission overseas. He went on to describe in detail about the visit of the fleet commander to the submarine and in a fearless tone opined, 'We should first trust our own officers and men till found otherwise rather than putting them on the chopping block without an iota of proof and expecting them to prove their innocence,' he summarized.

Admiral Thapar stayed silent till the XO completed his statement and exited the hall. Placing his pen on the table, he said, 'Gentlemen, I agree that we should avoid harassing our men. But the manner in which the CO and the XO have spoken gives an impression as if there's a revolt brewing on *Sindhkosh*. And that is even more alarming. I

agree that Gobind played the most crucial role in saving *Sindhkosh*, not once but twice. Yet, we must remember that we all work in a time-tested hierarchical system where the senior officer must be respected for his rank, authority and designation. Honest feedback is indeed desired but only so long as it remains within the four walls of discipline. Let's break for lunch.'

The board assembled again after the break and asked for Gobind to reappear. And soon as he sat down, the admiral took centre stage by firing at him a barrage of questions related to Taraa. Gobind kept responding at a matching pace till the admiral had nothing more to ask. Going against the protocol, the admiral allowed him to ask any question if he wished to, much to the surprise of all the members, but not before asking the steno to leave the hall.

'Sir,' began Gobind in a humble voice, 'Please accept my deep gratitude for giving me a patient hearing. I don't have any queries. I however wish to put it on record that I shall be seeking permission from the command to marry Taraa. Whatever recommendations, therefore, the BOI makes should be after taking this fact into consideration. I am fully devoted to my country. My commitment to my future wife cannot be a bargain for any decision that the board might take. Unfortunately, this was the one major issue that caused hurt to the fleet commander, which I deeply regret. I have nothing more to say, sir.'

'We do appreciate Lt Gobind Singh,' intervened the commodore. 'In fact, we appreciate you letting us know

your decision of marrying a Russian national. It clears the air of uncertainty in the minds of the members of the board. It's your personal choice. Besides, this glass ceiling must break, sooner than later. As regards to the rules, please rest assured that due justice shall prevail and the same shall emerge from our report, without any bias or prejudice. The board recognizes your service to the country, as also your professionalism, courage and truthfulness. But you must remember there is a lesson behind this incident that shall help you emerge stronger. We are sure you would learn a lot that shall hold you in good stead in future.' The board members nodded as the commodore finished his short speech and waited for his response.

'Sir,' began Gobind again after a pause. 'What I have learnt so far is that we are entering a new era where self-preservation is going to be the key to success. The world around us is focused on short-term goals and is willing to pay any price to achieve it. Gangway friendships that are temporary has become an accepted norm. We need to introspect. Indeed, this incident has come as a big lesson to me. I was expected to give up and bow down under the sheer weight of mental pressure. What I did at sea was what is expected of any submariner given the fact that we're trained and grilled to address such emergencies. I shall take it as a new beginning and build from here. Thank you so much for being patient and considerate.'

Admiral Thapar smiled as he stretched on the chair, visibly impressed by the young officer's maturity. There was a warmth-filled appreciative look on his face. 'You may

go back to *Sindhkosh* and resume your duty. All the best,' he concluded.

Gobind stood up and saluted smartly. He observed that the glittering steel shaft of the ceremonial golden butted sword lying in the centre of the long table in front was not pointing towards him, which as per the established naval customs meant that the board had come to a conclusion that he was not guilty. He looked at the commodore who smiled in return and gently blinked in reassurance. He walked past the row of officers, their eyes following him in admiration till he exited the hall. The tempo within the board room had changed quickly. All the officers were in a relaxed mood, which showed that a decision had been arrived at unanimously. The admiral stood up and carefully tucked his pen inside his shirt pocket. 'Call the steno,' he directed. 'Let's get done with this report.'

22

Admiral Bhaskar Rao was pacing up and down in his spacious office. A big, thick, unlit cigar hung loosely between his left hand's fingers. Held in his right hand was a thick, neatly coil-bound set of documents covered with a blue sheet, marked *confidential* in bold. Beneath the classification, it read *Board of Inquiry*. He walked up to the edge of his table and placed the report on it. He was about to light a cigar when the steward came in. 'Sir, CO *Sindhkosh* has arrived.' He placed the unlit cigar to top of the ashtray and sat down. 'Good. Please usher him in.'

Captain Sundaram Raju knocked gently but without waiting for a response pushed the door open. He made eye contact with the admiral while walking in a few steps and saluted. 'Come in, Raju; take a seat.' As the CO occupied the centre of the three chairs, he noticed the BOI report lying on the table. The steward walked in, served tea and left. The admiral waited till he heard a click, confirming

that the wooden door was shut tight. Lifting the cigar from the ashtray, he lit it with an expensive-looking lighter and took a few drags till its top end was burning brightly. Satisfied with his own performance, he gently placed the lighter on the table and looked at the captain questioningly. 'I am sure you have read this report too, Raju. What do you make of it?'

The CO was well aware of the reasons behind his summons to the fleet office, but he was not worried anymore. A strange sense of self belief had engulfed him. Having miraculously survived, he had realized that he owed his life and that of the entire crew to Gobind. His XO had further acted as a catalyst and had egged him to take a firm stand. 'Sir,' the XO had forcefully emphasized, 'The Command must know what's better for the navy. We know Gobind's integrity is above board. His professionalism is second to none. We should not let individual perceptions overrule reality. He is an asset to the submarine arm. And this fact is something that the headquarters must know directly from you.'

Placing the file on the table, the CO looked at the angry-faced fleet commander in front. 'Sir,' he began in a polite, soft voice. 'I have stated in my report as also deposed before the board of inquiry. In my capacity as the commanding officer of INS *Sindhkosh*, I have complete faith and confidence in Lt Gobind Singh and can vouch for his character, integrity and professional competence. With regards to his marriage to a foreign national, it is an individual decision for which the officer has already approached the command through

the proper channel.' Captain Raju paused briefly but found no change in the cold expressions on the fleet commander's face. Despite worries in his mind over the possible adverse reaction from his boss, he continued. 'Notwithstanding his decision to marry a foreigner, I have recommended that the headquarters should take into consideration his yeoman service, and that too at the very beginning of his career. I have stressed upon the need for him to be suitably rewarded instead of the command acting against him due to some frivolous and baseless complaint made by a disgruntled civilian in Leningrad.' The CO paused briefly again before continuing. With each passing moment he was becoming more determined to put forward his own observations without worrying about his own career or consequences.

'Sir, what Gobind has done has no parallel in the submarine arm history. It needs to be recognized. His act of bravado needs to be spread amongst all the submariners and widely spoken about to motivate others. Despite facing tough and challenging conditions, Gobind followed the emergency drill as if he had decades of hands-on experience in handling similar situations. He displayed a rare character of calm and composure. Completely isolated and locked in my cabin, I was but a mute listener, admiring the speed at which he rattled orders. His voice had a reassuring effect on the crew. His presence of mind was amazing. And his command and control on the drill was executed with impeccable precision. He was solely responsible for surfacing the submarine from a near-crushing depth. I, therefore, have the honour to recommend Lt Gobind

Singh's name for the highest Gallantry Award, the Veer Chakra, for saving *Sindhkosh* and its 100-member crew from sure-shot death. May I request you to accept the citation, sir?'

The admiral intently listened to the commanding officer in utter disbelief. He struggled with his cigar realizing the firmness with which the captain had expressed his opinion. Placing it haphazardly on the ash tray, spilling bits of ash on the table in the process, he stretched his right arm and accepted the documents. Before going through, he looked up at the captain again and hurriedly flipped through the pages till the end. The citation read more like a blue print of the emergency drill that INS *Sindhkosh* had undergone at sea.

The short, but powerfully worded report highlighted the stellar role young Gobind had played in saving the submarine. It recorded log reports and electronic data together with a synopsis of the actions taken for surfacing the submarine by the officer against all odds. The documents also carried official records of the then prevailing sea state, the weather conditions and a medical list of those injured on board, issued by the naval hospital. Sheepishly, he looked up again and, searching for the right words, managed to say, 'How I wish you had brought all these details to my knowledge well in time, Raju. Indeed, I was upset with Gobind's conduct during my visit on board. But you should have put forth your viewpoint then. Anyhow, leave this with me. Let me see how the situation can be retrieved.'

'Oh, thank you sir,' replied the beaming CO while saluting. 'You standing by him at this hour of his need shall go a long way in addressing many issues. It shall also have a positive effect on the morale of my officers and men on board. I am so grateful.' As the CO opened the door to exit the fleet commander's office, he saw the flag lieutenant rushing in with a note book in hand.

'Yes, sir,' said the officer while rushing up to the table and coming to a hurried halt.

'Flags, please make an RTC to C-in-C West.' (RTC stands for 'Request time convenient to call on you', which the Fleet Commander sent to the Commander in Chief of the Western Naval Command).

'Aye, aye, sir,' said the flag lieutenant and rushed back to comply.

23

Sunday morning was a holiday for most of the naval fraternity. But the Western Naval Officer's Command Mess was humming with activity. Dressed in white formal uniforms, officers had begun assembling on the lawns facing the Arabian Sea at the back of the complex. Right from the entrance gate over a 100 metres away, both sides of the long driveway were decorated with ceremonial life buoys hung from tall wooden cross stands. Each life buoy belonged to the naval ships, submarines and establishments operating under the Western Naval Command. Smartly dressed sentries, buglers and the naval band were in position to welcome the arriving guests. Tens of round tables dressed with white cloth and red roses covered most of the cemented quarter deck. Next to the reception desk inside, a placard read in bold words, 'Official function to celebrate the wedding reception of Lt Gobind Singh and Mrs Taraa Karamanov Singh'.

After handing over the peak cap at the reception desk, every officer stood for a brief moment and re-read the notice on the board. And, without exception, everyone had the same question in mind. 'How did he get this permission?' Amidst the growing hush-hush discussions amongst the officers, the sound of the bugle forewarned every one of the arrival of the commander-in-chief (C-in-C), Vice Admiral Arjun Singh. As the car stopped, he alighted and removed his peak cap. Rear Admiral Bhaskar Rao saluted and received the C-in-C, while the commander at arms took the cap and handed it over to the sailor on duty for safe custody.

Shaking hands with the fleet commander, the C-in-C stopped briefly and smiling said, 'Bhaskar, do you understand, we have set up a new protocol for this officer of yours? Not only has the naval headquarters accorded permission to Lt Gobind Singh to marry a foreigner, but it has also concurred for the wedding ceremony to take place in the command mess, something which till yesterday was considered impossible.'

'Thank you, sir. It's a fine gesture on the NHQ's part, especially when taking into account Gobind's exceptional service in saving so many lives as also a brand-new submarine.'

The C-in-C nodded in agreement and entered the big reception hall.

The ceremony began as soon as the master of the ceremonies received the signal from the master at arms. By the time the admiral took his seat on the plush white sofa, the band was in its full flow, playing to the delight of

the audience. Dressed in a smart, Chinese-collared white tunic (called the No 2s) studded with golden stripes, brass buttons and a shiny ceremonial sword, Gobind stood at the designated spot and waited. Ranjit, Amrita, Ram Dyal and Bihari Lal arrived together and were escorted by Muthu to the sofas in front. Wearing a grey suit with a matching tie, Bihari Lal proudly walked in front as if he was giving away his own daughter Meera. A few minutes later, Taraa came in, holding her father Karamanov's arm. From top to bottom, she was covered in a tightly fitting white silk gown. Her hair was tied in a bun, adorned with tiny fresh white flowers, which loosely hung at the back. She looked like a fairy who had stepped on the earth for a very special occasion.

The two looked at each other and smiled. Taraa took a step forward and held Gobind's hand. The grand audience of navy officers in crisp white ceremonial uniforms and the beautifully dressed ladies began applauding simultaneously. Dozens of hands raised a toast, each holding a champagne glass. The naval band began playing the music adding a new dimension to the starry, all-navy show. Not to be left behind, Karamanov took the centre stage and began swinging in a typical Russian step-dance to the rousing claps of guests. On top of the hut near the ocean, a big brass bell tolled aloud, one gong at a time, while a video clip of the two getting formally married in a gurudwara played in the background. In that ceremony, Taraa was dressed in a bright red traditional attire, the salwar-suit and embroidered dupatta. She slowly walked behind

her husband as the singers sang the shloka '*Har chouthri lanwa* . . .' They bowed in front of the holy book after each round and were declared married after the fourth round. Held firmly in her hands was the deity (Krishna) that Meera had left behind for Gobind.

As if on cue, the officers quickly assembled on each side of the carpet in a single line and raised their swords diagonally. Right through the reception hall till the waiting white ambassador car Gobind and Taraa walked in between the canopy of the steel shafts pointing skywards. Dressed almost identically were the bridesmaids, Tanya and Veronica, who walked behind at a short distance. And giving them company was none other than Muthu, constantly speaking to Taraa in Russian, urging her to pair him up with one of the bridesmaids. The C-in-C and his wife, the First Lady, stood at the end. She held the bride's hands, admiring Taraa's beauty. 'Welcome to the family. I must admit that your dear husband has faced many a storm to marry you. Very courageous indeed. And so very romantic. Wish you a long, smooth and an even keel sailing ahead.'

'Thank you so much, Ma'am. We are indeed grateful. Perhaps this storm was an important part of our lives. For we now know who held our hand and who let it go while we ran this marathon,' replied Taraa softly, leaving the First Lady completely floored. She held Taraa's hands, admiring her gown and jewellery and complimenting her looks and beauty.

A happy Ram Dyal thanked the admiral for the best wedding he had ever seen. Bihari Lal, Amrita and Ranjit

stood with joined palms. The couple walked slowly till they faced Bihari Lal. Taraa looked at Gobind to reconfirm and then bowed to touch his feet. The village head was taken by complete surprise and was overwhelmed by her gesture. Putting his hands on her head, he blessed her profusely. 'I was told that you resemble my daughter Meera. Looking at you, it appears as if my little angel has forgiven me and has come back home. Your haveli in Bihar eagerly awaits you and my son-in-law.'

A visibly happy C-in-C joined in and addressed his four special guests from Bihar. 'Sir, my wife and I shall be highly obliged if you could kindly join us for dinner tonight in the honour of the bride and the groom.' Ranjit looked flabbergasted. Overwhelmed by the humble tone of the C-in-C, he somehow managed to say, 'Sir, we are poor people. I am a small-time farmer who works as a daily wager. We are not fit to be your guests.'

The admiral smiled and turned to face Ranjit and Amrita. 'Sir, a farmer's son from Bihar has saved over a 100 naval lives. The noble school headmaster from Patna taught him how to stand firmly and speak the truth and only the whole truth. I wish there were many more Gobinds. It will be our honour to receive you. We shall wait for you, sir.'

The First Lady too joined in. Looking at Amrita, she politely inquired, 'What kind of food do you like, Ma'am?' Amrita hesitated, looked at her husband and somehow managed to say, 'Ji, we are vegetarians. Just a simple meal will do. Thank you so much.' The First Lady stepped forward and hugged Amrita while the admiral gestured

to his staff. 'Flags, please escort our guests to navy house at 2000 hours.' The young lieutenant sprang into action. 'Aye, aye, sir,' he said and saluted in acknowledgement.

Together, they walked towards the main porch while the naval police swiftly moved to the line-up of vehicles in the order of seniority. But the C-in-C wasn't done yet. In yet another rare gesture, he escorted the young bride to her car, opened the door and waited till she settled down inside. Both he and his wife then waved at the newlyweds as their car sped away. Together, they then saw off Ranjit Singh's family who were escorted to the VIP suite at the palatial Western Naval Command Mess. Amrita entered the spacious suite and opened her bag. Gently and respectfully taking the picture frame of her deity out of her bag, she carefully placed it on the table and stood in front while Ranjit took his position on the side. Joining their palms, they sat down on the floor and prayed. Their lips were in complete sync with that of each other. 'Thank you, Gobind, for standing by our Gobind.' Their eyes were shut; they couldn't see an unmistakable smile on the deity's face.

Epilogue

Gobind received the gallantry award, the Veer Chakra. He took premature retirement as lieutenant commander.

Taraa took Indian citizenship and shifted to Patna with Gobind.

Bihari Lal formally adopted Taraa as his daughter and bequeathed his entire property in her name, and Taraa converted the residential palace into the 50-bed Meera Charitable Hospital. The two pillars at the entry gate were named after Hira-Moti.

Ranjit and Amrita set up a free education centre in the village and named it the Patna Sahib Public School. Ram Dyal Sharma became its chairman. It now has over 100 bright students.

Commodore Biswal was court-martialled and removed from service.

The Russian Government sacked Sergei and imprisoned him for trying to bribe an Indian Navy officer.

Acknowledgements

Cheena, Puneet, Samar and Simba.

Wg. Cdr. Unni Kartha (Retd.), NDA (37th Course).

Cmde. Aspi Cawasji (Retd.) and my coursemates (5719).

Tarun Ishwa, for the cover photograph.

I am grateful to Rahul Nanda for always standing by me and being forthcoming with his expert advice and guidance.